ROGUES TO RICHES

Also by Jerri Kay Lincoln:

Rutledge Historical Society Cozy Mysteries
Message for Murder
Death over Divorce
Kousins Kan't Kill
Rogues to Riches
Secrets for Sale

Memoir
The Dog Who Rescued Me

Children's Books
Cooper's Smile
The Little Unicorn Who Could
Do Bears Poop in the Woods?
Can Pigs Fly?
Why Do Puppy Dogs Have Cold Noses?
The Invisible Lion
La Petite Licorne Qui Pouvait
Das Kleine Einhorn Was Es Kann
The Little Unicorn Who Could Coloring Book
Do Bears Poop in the Woods? Coloring Book

Cookbooks
Ten Delicious Dairy-Free Stevia-Sweetened Ice Cream
Recipes

Rogues to Riches

Jerri Kay Lincoln

Ralston Store Publishing
P.O. Box 1684
Prescott, Arizona 86302

ISBN 978-1-938322-52-5

Professionally edited by:
Jennifer Hope
www.MesaVerdeMediaServices.com

The reader should note that the nutritional beliefs and food choices in this book are those of the characters and not necessarily those of the author or publisher.

Dedicated to the sleuth in all of us.

CHAPTER ONE

THE WINDOW IN front of the large wooden desk that I sat at needed cleaning, both inside and out. But I wouldn't do it now. I had worked at the Rutledge Historical Society for a few months shy of a year. They used to hire out the cleaning, but I didn't mind doing it myself. Today, though, I was too nervous to do it. If I had boots on, I'd be shaking in them. But I had heels on. I always had heels on. And heels don't lend themselves to shaking in, so I decided to bite my fingernails instead. But I've never done that, so I needed to think of something else to ease my anxiety.

My dog Bingo was at my feet. Bingo is a Cavalier King Charles Spaniel. Mostly black and white, he has tan eyebrows and a touch of tan on each cheek that makes him look like he has rouge on. I almost lost him, but I felt grateful that I had him now. He knew I was upset—he always knew. That was one of the things that makes dogs so awesome. They *know* you—better than anyone else. And they know what to do to make you feel better. To say that dogs give you unconditional love is like saying that icebergs are kinda big under the water. Dogs give so much more than just unconditional love. Although Bingo's presence made me feel better, it was not enough to get me through this trial.

Wednesday was usually hump day, but today was *terror* day. I was scared to death. I'd never felt so frightened in my entire life—or at least it felt that way at the moment. The really bad and sad part was that I couldn't confide in *anyone* about what was happening. And it wasn't just the fright—it was the shame.

What could my son have done to cause the principal, Pamela Reilly—whom I had considered a friend—to write me such a business-like formal letter stating that she needed to talk to me about Aiden? He was such a good kid, I couldn't imagine what he might have done. Had he hit another student? That wasn't like Aiden at all. Had he yelled at a teacher? Aiden would never do that. Did he cheat? Aiden was so far ahead in his class that he had no need to cheat. Or was that maybe the way he had gotten so far ahead? No way. The kid read adult level books—he *earned* his way to the top of his class. So what could it be?

Taking a deep breath, I tried to calm myself and think positive thoughts. How bad could a seven-year-old be? And the good part about this day was that after it was all over, I could finally tell Billy about it. Billy was my boyfriend—no wait—he was my fiancé. He had asked me to marry him at Thanksgiving, after which we both decided to wait until after the holidays to plan anything.

Now it was the second week of January, and I'd been putting Billy off for more than a week now. He had probably been thinking that I'd changed my mind. Once the meeting is over, then I'll tell him. That's what I'd been telling myself, but if it's something horrible, then what? I was in the middle of adopting Aiden, and the plan was that Billy would adopt him, too. So if Aiden did something really horrible, then maybe Billy wouldn't want to adopt him. He is the county sheriff and has an image to maintain. Maybe he wouldn't want to marry me! Aiden and I were a package deal, after all.

I took another deep breath and tried to think of the positive—you know, lemonade out of lemons and all that. The unknown is worse than the known. Whatever Aiden had done, I would deal with it. And I would confess my deception to Billy. If there's one thing I know about Billy, it's that he is understanding. We would deal with Aiden's transgression together, because that's what couples do. It would be all right. I knew it would be. Kind of.

"Hey, Lorry," called Petra. "What are you still doing at your desk? Did Martha send over more typing or something?" Petra was the sixteen-year-old girl I worked with. She was weird weird weird to the max. With her purple hair, multiple piercings, and multiple tattoos, Petra looked like she should be on some street corner begging for money for drugs or alcohol. At least that's what I used to think.

Petra was my first lesson in assuming and judging. And I needed a lot of lessons. Still. Because Petra was one of the most responsible, reliable, solid people that I had ever met. I couldn't respect her any more than I already do. And did I mention that she was completing her last two years of high school and first two years of college online? That's why she spent days with me at the historical society—working on her studies. She only *really* worked in the morning before her studies began and in the afternoons when school would traditionally be out.

The *Martha* she mentioned was Martha Goldstein, our boss. When I first started at the society, I did a lot of typing for her, but in the last couple of months she had learned to type. Now my main work was scanning all the historical documents that were upstairs in boxes. And I should be up there now instead of fidgeting at my desk—hence Petra's question.

"Um, no, Petra, I need to leave in a minute or two, so I didn't think it was worth starting the scanning. But don't worry, I'll put the sign out." The historical society had been really busy since we had the new exhibit up. It was about an unsolved murder in Rutledge in the fifties. Aiden wanted to solve it.

"No need. I don't mind people coming in. They usually don't need an official tour. Where are you going?"

Without answering, I grabbed the sign and my purse from my desk drawer and opened the front door. Although Petra had said not to put the sign up, I moved the hands so that the sign said *Back at 10:00*. "I'll be back soon, Petra! See ya! Bingo, stay!" And I walked out into the bright morning sunshine.

It may have been bright and sunshiny, but it wasn't warm. Unfortunately, in my hurry to *escape*, I had left my jacket on my chair. It may be Arizona, but winter in the Arizona mountains could be chilly. And to prove my point, *a chill wind* blew through my clothes and made me shiver. This time, it was from the cold and not from fright.

Since I had left a few minutes earlier than I had intended, I needed to waste some time before my nine-thirty appointment. I didn't want to get to the school any earlier than I had to. So instead of going on the side of the historical building which was faster, I decided to walk all the way around the block, past the library, the sheriff's station—where Billy worked—and then down the street to the school at the end of the block. My steps quickened as I passed the sheriff's office, because I didn't want Billy to see me.

I arrived at Aiden's school at nine-twenty-five, hoping to talk to Marylou before seeing the principal. She maybe could give me information on Aiden's indiscretion or indiscretions, before I had to face Pamela. Marylou had been a fixture at the school from the time when I went to school there. She was one of my favorite people on earth. But after Marylou and I hugged, Pamela came to the door—smiling—inviting me into her office. Smiling? What was that about?

I was wearing my beige pantsuit with beige heels to match. And I can't tell you what Pamela was wearing, because it was all I could do to keep blinking away the tears that kept wanting to form in my eyes.

Pamela must have noticed that something was wrong, because she put her hand on my arm. "Lorry, what's wrong? Is everything okay?"

Sniffling, I said, "It's all right, Pamela. You can tell me what he did. I can take it."

She looked at me quizzically. "Um, what who did?"

"Aiden! Isn't that why you wrote me that official-looking letter to come see you? Because Aiden did something horribly wrong?"

She put her hand back on my arm and tried unsuccessfully to stifle a laugh. "Oh, Lorry. You thought that letter was something bad?" When I nodded, she continued, "I never thought to mention that those letters go out to *all* the students' parents every year just after

5

New Year's. The kindergartener letters are slightly different—they explain that it's our policy to meet with every parent to give them an update on how their child is doing. Not only so they have some idea before report cards, but also, if there is a problem, maybe they can resolve the issue."

Pamela shook her head and looked at me. "But Aiden is a dream! He hasn't done anything wrong. You should know that, Lorry."

After a week of thinking the worst about Aiden, now knowing that he had done nothing wrong made the tears stream down my face. "I should have known, I know," I nodded my head as I spoke. "But the letter looked so official, and it scared me so much. I didn't even tell Billy!"

"Billy? Ah, the sheriff?"

"Yes, my fiancé." Looking up, I said, "You know Billy?"

She laughed again. "Since Thanksgiving, Aiden has been repeatedly telling everyone that he will soon be the *sheriff's* son."

Despite the tears dripping down my face, I had to laugh. "He's really been doing that?"

"Oh, yeah. He's very proud of that."

As I walked back to the office with a huge smile on my face, I felt guilty not only for leaving Billy out of Aiden's and my *problem*, but for the way I had treated Aiden since I had received the letter. Although I had done all the *motherly* actions required of me, my heart wasn't in it. Not only could I not make eye contact with him, but when I hugged him it was like that experiment where they gave baby monkeys a *mother* made out of wire. The baby monkeys didn't exactly thrive under those conditions.

That's what I had been the past week—a mother made out of wire.

It's not something I was proud of—I'm admitting it out of shame and guilt. And I assure you that I never once considered stopping the adoption procedures—it was just that I had no idea how to proceed when I started having doubts about someone whom I had thought was incredible. I didn't know how I would make it up to Aiden, but I would. He had been asking me if something was wrong, because he's such an astute kid, and I had been putting him off. He had let it go, but sometimes I saw him looking at me funny when he didn't think I was watching. And Billy! I had put him off so long about wedding plans, he probably thought I wanted to call off the engagement.

When I reached the door of the historical society, a woman in a walker, with an oxygen tank hanging off it, was pounding on the door. She said, "What does this sign mean? Back at 10:00? I thought it opened at 9:00!"

Unlocking the door, I said, "It does. But I had a meeting at my son's school. Sorry." I opened the door, stepped in, and held it open for her. Since I remembered her yelling at me when she had visited here a few months before, I didn't offer to help.

Wearing an expensive blue and white striped pantsuit and matching old lady shoes, she struggled through the doorway and thumped down the hallway toward the new exhibit. As the front door jingled as it opened again, I heard her call from the back room, "I *told* you that you're missing two of the suspects!"

A woman—I recognized her from when she accompanied her mother before—walked in stooped over with her hand on her belly. She wore an expensive suit that I suspected she had made just for her, although it was hard to tell because of the way she stood bent over like that. "I was going to ask if my mother was here, but I see—I mean hear—that she is." She shook her head. "I have some kind of stomach thing going on and was only in the bathroom five minutes when she disappeared from next door." Shaking her head again, she looked at me, frowned, motioned toward her mother, and continued, "Nobody signs up for this." Not saying anything more, she walked down the hallway. "Come on, Mother. You don't belong here."

"Then where do I belong? Huh? Tell me that, Jacqueline!" By this time, they were by the door, and the old woman looked at me. "I told you *last time* I was here that you didn't have all the suspects up there! And do you fix it? No!"

The daughter frowned at me and said, "I'm sorry," and escorted her mother out the door.

Bingo, not used to the yelling, pressed up against my legs. I patted him and called out, "Did you hear that, Petra?" When she didn't answer, I walked into her office to tell her the story about Aiden, but she was on the phone with her boyfriend Mason. I knew that because she was faced toward her computer and talking in hushed tones, which is how she always talked to Mason. Returning to my desk, I popped my purse into the bottom drawer and was getting ready to head upstairs with Bingo when a crowd of people came in and rushed past me.

Shrugging, I was about to follow them on my way upstairs, when someone pounded on the door again. It was the old woman, returned. I opened the door for her and watched her thump her way down the hallway toward the exhibit again. Her daughter would probably be coming in right after her, but I needed to get to work, so I walked quickly up the stairs. The daughter would know how to find her.

The group of people were still crowded around the new exhibit, but I heard the old woman say, "Make way! Make way! I can't see over your ugly heads! Move over and let an old woman see in there."

Since I heard nothing else from the old woman but some grumbling, I assumed they had moved over for her. I turned on the computer and the scanner preparing to start my work. Several minutes later, I heard multiple sets of footsteps receding down the hallway. The group had left. Then the old woman said, "Hey, you up there! When are you going to fix your rogue's gallery down here? You're missing two suspects—a man *and* a woman! And there's something else about this exhibit that you've got wrong! That gun is not the murder—what! *You!*"

And then a shot rang out.

CHAPTER TWO

BINGO, LYING AT my feet, barked. I shuddered. The shot was unsettling and surprising, yes. What really disturbed me, though, were the sounds that followed: a body falling to the floor along with a large piece of light metal and the clunk of what could only have been the oxygen tank, the smash of something against the hard plastic of the exhibit, then the footsteps running toward the back, and the sound of the back door slamming.

I knew what awaited me at the bottom of the stairs: another dead body. Too many bodies were piling up at the foot of these stairs—it was like the stairs were haunted or something. Maybe I needed to get someone in here to exorcise them. Or something.

As I hurried down the stairs in my heels, rushing as fast as I could but stopping short of taking two stairs at a time, Petra yelled to me, "Lorry, come quick! Someone shot the old woman!"

When I reached the bottom of the stairs, I saw the old woman's walker turned over and the oxygen tank lying on the floor. She was lying on her back, with her eyes open, a surprised look on her face, and a hole in her chest that was leaking blood.

"I'll call an ambulance!" said Petra, running back to her desk.

Kneeling down, I put my hand on the woman's neck and felt for a pulse. She looked deader than a squished fly, but I might as well do everything nice and proper-like. Her pulse was thready. I wasn't sure what that meant, but I could barely feel the pulse, and I thought that must be what it meant.

Standing up, I called out, "Call Billy, too, Petra. I'm no doctor, but I don't think this woman is going to make it. She probably needs a hearse, not an ambulance." The bullet hole was between her breasts, so it probably went through her heart. Blood was appearing on her lips, so the bullet must have nicked her lung, too. Poor old woman. I knelt down by her side again. Her eyes blinked once, and a weird sound escaped her bloody lips. When I put my fingers to her neck again to check the pulse, it wasn't there. She was gone.

Although I didn't hesitate to put my fingers on her neck, putting my fingers on her eyes to close them grossed me out. Or maybe it was because she was alive before, and now she was for sure dead. I don't know, I just know I couldn't do it.

Thankfully, Billy walked in then. It was more like he stormed in from the back door. When he saw the old woman, he knelt down and put his fingers to her neck feeling for the same pulse that I couldn't find. He shook his head. "She's gone." Then he reached out and closed both of her eyes using his thumb and forefinger. Being a sheriff, he was used to dead bodies—especially since *I*

11

had moved back to town. Dead bodies seemed to follow me.

Petra stood in the hallway by her desk, too far away to see anything clearly. Billy stood up and said, "I don't suppose either of you saw what happened here."

I frowned and shook my head. Petra said, "Lorry was upstairs, and I was at my desk. There were a group of people in here and then it sounded like they all left. Next thing I heard was the old woman saying something, and then I heard the shot."

"Did you get a good look at the group of people?"

"I didn't," said Petra.

Shaking my head, I said, "No, I didn't, either. They were six or seven business people, some young, some old. Nondescript."

"What was the old woman saying before you heard the shot?" Billy asked.

"Something about a rogue's gallery and missing suspects and—"

But I didn't get to finish because the front bell jingled, and the younger woman walked in, her hand still on her belly, and she called out, "Mother! What are you—"

I yelled out, "Petra!" so she could stop the woman from coming in the back and stumbling on her mother's dead body.

Petra said soothing words to the woman too quiet for me to hear. But the woman said, "No!" in a loud voice. "I want to see her!"

Billy and I stepped aside to give the woman room. She knelt down by her mother's side and said, "Oh, Mother, oh, Mother. Why couldn't you leave it alone?" As she ran her hand along her mother's head that was sparsely covered in gray hair, she kept repeating, "Oh, Mother, oh, Mother." Then she abruptly stood up and grabbed her stomach. "The bathroom? Quick! Where's the bathroom?"

She slammed the door without locking it, and what followed were disgusting and rude noises. Billy and I looked at each other. I tried to suppress it, but I couldn't help myself, and I started to giggle. When Billy gave me a dirty look, I bit my lip. It was wrong of me to laugh, I know. The poor woman's mother had just died. But I can be irreverent at times, and frankly, I think that's one of my assets.

"Lorry, honestly," Petra said from her office, "you can be so childish." She paused and went on, "Childish. Old English from the early fifteenth century, meaning puerile, immature, like a child."

Frowning, Billy said, "Yeah, that fits."

I was about to stomp off in a pretend huff, but I heard the ambulance drive up to the back of the historical society. Billy heard it, too, and ran to the back—definitely faster than I could have gotten there in my heels.

The woman came out of the bathroom and said, "I'm sorry about," she motioned with her head toward the bathroom, "but I'm really sick and have been since last night, but Mother insisted on coming to the cafe today." She took a quick look at her mother and blew her a kiss. "I'm going home now."

"I think Billy will want to talk to you," I told her.

She dug in her purse and handed me a card. It said *Jacqueline Pennington, Real Estate Agent*, and gave her address and phone number. With her hand still on her stomach, she said, "I'm still sick. I need to get home. Have him call me. Sorry." And with a frown on her face,

Jerri Kay Lincoln

she stole another quick glance at her mother and hurried
out the front door.

CHAPTER THREE

BILLY LED THE paramedics, carrying a stretcher, from the back. He looked around. "Where is the daughter?"

"She had to leave. But she gave me her card." When I went to hand it to him, I realized there were two cards stuck together, so I handed him one and kept the other one.

Billy looked at the card, read the name aloud, "Jacqueline Pennington," and then stuck it in his pocket. Nick, Billy's deputy, had followed the paramedics in and was making the most of the crime scene by smearing fingerprint powder all over everything he could think of. He must have already done the back door, because he had a smudge of it on his cheek.

Billy frowned while the paramedics examined the body. Although I hadn't even worked at the historical society a full year, I had already seen multiple dead bodies and had almost been one myself more than once. So I walked to my desk and sat down, so I wouldn't have to watch the procedure—whatever the procedure was. I didn't want to know. After dropping the card into my top desk drawer, I started surfing the 'net. I wouldn't be getting any work done with all the excitement down the hallway.

When I heard the back door close, I knew the dead body and its attendants had left. I wasn't sure about Billy, though, until I heard his footsteps returning from the back door. "Lor," he called out, "can you come here a sec?"

Walking to the back, I saw the walker, now upright, and Billy standing next to it. The oxygen tank had disappeared. The paramedics must have taken it in case the woman sprung to life. Or something.

"You were upstairs, right?" Not waiting for me to answer, Billy continued, "What did you hear?"

"A shot. A body hitting the floor, the walker and the oxygen tank hitting the floor, and a smashing sound." I turned around to look at the new exhibit that everyone in town was coming in to see. The exhibit was intact. "But I don't see any cracks in the plastic."

"Oh, you won't." Billy ran his hand along the plastic door of the exhibit. "This is a special kind of plastic. It's Lexan. It's like bulletproof glass." He continued running his hand along the door. "Ah, here. Feel this." Pointing to the plastic, he took my hand in his and pushed my finger into a small dent. "It won't crack or shatter, but it dings and scratches easily."

Still holding onto my hand, he peered into the exhibit —at the gun. "That's probably what whoever did this wanted. But why kill the old woman? Why not wait until she had left? That makes no sense."

"Oh! That reminds me! She said something right before she was shot. She said something like *That's not the murder—you!*"

16

"What does that mean? 'That's not the murder you.' I don't get it."

I looked down at the gun. "She must have been talking about the gun not being the murder—*weapon*, I guess. And someone, the *you* she was talking about, was someone she knew who interrupted her."

Billy nodded. "That sounds logical. I'll have to think about this before I call Jacqueline Pennington." Then he looked down the hallway and whispered, "Petra in there?" When I nodded, he firmly grasped my hand, which he had never let go of, and gently pulled me into the back room by the door.

"I have to ask you something, Lorry."

Shrugging, I said, "Okay." We were way past him thinking I killed anybody, so I knew it wasn't that.

He looked into my eyes, and I noticed that his eyes were moist. "Do you still want to marry me or have you changed your mind? Because every time I want to make plans, you change the subject."

"Oh, Billy!" I threw my arms around him and plastered his face with kisses. "Of course I still want to marry you! I *love* you!" With all the excitement, I had forgotten all about my fright this morning and how I had been treating both Billy and Aiden. "I'm sorry. I'll explain everything, honest I will, just not now."

He kissed me back and then put both hands on my shoulders. "But whatever it is, it has to do with Aiden, too, right? Because he asked me if maybe you had decided not to adopt him."

I put my head in my hands and once again felt like the bad mommy of the month. I knew what I had been doing and felt bad about it, but finding out that Aiden not only noticed but talked to Billy about it broke my heart. Of course Aiden had noticed—just like Billy noticed. They were both very sensitive *men*. "Yes, it involves Aiden, and I want to tell you separately from him. Maybe you can help me figure out a way to tell him that doesn't make me sound like a horrible mother."

"Oh, Lorry. You're not a horrible mother, and you know that Aiden never thinks that."

"I don't know. Sometimes I feel like that, and in this case, I definitely think it's justified. Wait till you hear what happened. You'll agree with me. I'm an awful mother."

Billy put his hands on his hips and shook his head. "All right, tell me. I'm listening."

"Not now! It's complicated," I said. Although when I thought about it, it didn't seem that complicated at all.

"Come on, tell me now. Get it over with. Let me decide."

"No, Billy, I'm not telling you now." Looking up at him, I crossed my arms in front of my chest, and just for effect, I stuck out my lower lip in a pout. Yes, I can be stubborn and petulant, but Billy loves me anyway.

CHAPTER FOUR

BILLY KNEW BETTER than to try to get it out of me, so we agreed that we would go out to lunch and I would tell him then. At first, we thought I could just leave work early, that wouldn't work, though, because Aiden walked over to the society after school. So lunch it was.

After moving the woman's walker to the back room out of the way, I retired upstairs to continue with my scanning. When lunchtime came, we ended up ordering Chinese and eating it at my house, for privacy. I wasn't prepared to bare my soul in front of the general population. Just saying it in front of Billy would be difficult enough. And I even made Billy wait until after we finished eating. Billy thought I was giving him a bad time until I explained that it was hard enough for me to confess, but I didn't want to do it while I was eating. That was true, but I also didn't want to bare my soul and eat with my mouth open at the same time. That just grossed me out.

So there we were, sitting on the couch with Billy's arm tight around me—he knew I needed that—and me confessing how stupid I was. Although it wasn't easy telling him everything like that, it made both of us feel better. Billy, because I didn't want to back out of the upcoming marriage, and me, because after hearing it, *Billy* didn't want to back out of the upcoming marriage.

"Lorry, it's understandable. You've never received a letter like that, and you had no way to know that was the protocol and that *everyone* got the letter."

I sighed, heavily. "You're being too understanding."

"No, I'm not, because I'm about to reprimand you."

Pulling away from his embrace, I narrowed my eyes and looked at him. "*You're* going to reprimand *me*? What right do you have—" I sank back into his arms and rested my head on his chest. "Oh, wait, you do. Go ahead. I deserve it."

"First, you should know that *our* Aiden," he emphasized our, "would never do anything that would require a parent/principal meeting—unless it was something outstanding. He's not perfect, but he's got a good head on his shoulders. *You* know that."

I nodded, but felt like he wasn't through with me yet. "Yes, I know."

"But the big thing is that you kept a *secret* from me. A *big* secret. And had you confided in me, I could have relieved your worry. You wouldn't have had to put me and Aiden off for the last week. That was bad. I don't believe in secrets between two people who love each other." Billy leaned over and kissed my cheek to soften the reprimand. But I deserved all of it. Then he continued. "So let's make an agreement right now—no more secrets. Okay?" He smiled gently at me and then kissed me on the lips. "There we go, sealed with a kiss." Then he pulled his arm away, coughed, looked into the distance, and wrapped his arm back around me.

20

I snuggled deeper into him. "Okay, it's a deal. What am I going to tell Aiden?"

"Don't worry about it. I'll talk to Aiden." Billy gave me a squeeze, kissed my cheek, pulled his arm away, and stood up. "All right, we're going in the right direction now—which is good because Martha and Hugo invited us to dinner tonight to talk about the wedding. And now I have to leave to work on this new murder case." He turned and headed toward the door.

"Billy, wait! What time do we have to be at Martha and Hugo's? Will we have time to talk to Aiden first? I'd really like to get that over with."

He opened the front door, and I followed him out. "Five-thirty. I'll meet you here at five, so we can talk to Aiden together. Follow my lead."

"Wait! Doesn't Aiden have karate tonight?"

"Nope. Instructor's on vacation for a couple of weeks."

Giving me a quick peck on the lips, he strode toward his car, all six feet four inches of him. I was so lucky to have him and so lucky that he was—mostly— understanding of my actions of the previous week. My reprimand was well deserved, and mostly, he took my transgressions well. Of course I shouldn't have been afraid at all. Aiden was a great kid. Not only would he not do anything bad worth a parent/teacher conference, but Pamela Reilly was my friend. If by a million to one chance Aiden *did* do something bad, she would *call* me. Simple as that. And keeping a secret like that from Billy? I'm not only the bad mommy of the month, but I'm the bad fiancée of the month. Color me ashamed. Very, very ashamed.

21

Jerri Kay Lincoln

No use fretting over it now. I cleaned up the scant mess we made, freshened up in the powder room, and took off for the historical society, Bingo in tow. When I walked in the back door and started down the hallway, Petra said, "You had a visitor."

CHAPTER FIVE

FROM THE DESCRIPTION that Petra gave me, it sounded like Sam, my old friend from high school who had recently moved back to town. Sam had said she'd return the following day to talk to me. As I walked to my desk, Petra called me back.

"Hey, that reminds me, did I hear Billy say the name Pennington this morning?"

"Yeah. That's the name of the woman whose mother got killed back there."

Petra had a funny look on her face. "You know, Lorry, that's really weird. Pennington is the name of the guy who was killed."

"Guy who was killed. What are you talking about? What guy?"

"You know! Edward!"

"Petra, you're talking in circles. Who is Edward and when was he killed? I have my hands full with the old woman in the walker."

"The exhibit, Lorry! The exhibit! Edward is the one who was killed in the exhibit!"

"What? Exhibit? I still—" And then it occurred to me. "*Who killed Edward?*" I said, finally understanding what Petra was trying to tell me. "That murder was what, in the fifties? And now here is his—what? She must be his granddaughter, right? And here she is practically on the scene of the crime. That's a little too convenient, isn't it, Petra?" Without waiting for an answer, I continued, "And whoever killed the old woman, tried to get into the exhibit, too. There's a little dent in the door from where she whacked it."

"She?"

"Well, you know, if Jacqueline Pennington killed her own mother . . ."

"Now, Lorry, don't go making conclusions based on insufficient evidence, *again*. I thought you'd learned that lesson already. Just because the woman's name is the same doesn't mean that she is related to Edward Pennington and *certainly* doesn't mean that she killed her mother. It might even be her married name."

"I know, I know," I said, a little impatient with Petra's criticisms. Just because they were well-founded didn't mean they didn't bother me. That made them bother me and annoy me even more. "But it's a place to start."

"What are you going to do? I thought you'd stop this investigating once you got married. To the sheriff, I might add."

From the other room, I said, "I'm not married, yet. Right?" Then I dug out the card from my drawer and held it up. "I'm going to call her, but not yet. First," I headed toward the back, "I want to investigate the original murder. They must be connected!"

As Bingo and I walked up the stairs, I heard Petra say in an exasperated tone, "Oh, Lorry!"

The first thing I did was move the *Children* binder that I was currently working on to scan all the documents inside. After Thanksgiving, I had started with *Automobiles* when Aiden and I had finished putting together the new exhibit. But with all the holiday time off and my other duties, I hadn't gotten very far with the binders. It was slow going. Not only did I scan each document, but I also had to organize and cross-reference everything.

I set the *Children* binder against the wall next to the scanner and then walked to the shelves that held the other binders. Since I had put them all away, I knew exactly where the binder I was looking for was. Stepping up to it, I pulled it off the shelf. "Right here," I said to myself, since even Bingo wasn't listening, "here's what I want." There were three binders called *Police Beat*, each one divided into years. With an educated guess, I selected the middle one, and guessed right. Quite satisfied with myself, I patted myself on the back—metaphorically speaking, of course—and returned to the computer and scanner setup.

Zackary James, former juvenile delinquent, former jailbird, and one of my favorite people, did the setup for me. I did what I could, but Zack knew how to get it exactly how I wanted it. Had I tried to figure it out for myself, it would have taken me a lot longer than it took him. Zack works for the post office and takes college classes at night, so I figured he could use the money.

Sitting down at my desk, I started leafing through the binder. Since I had already experienced the haphazard placement of documents in the binders, I knew better than to expect the 1950s to be in chronological order. And I was right. Not only that, but when I glanced through the sixties and forties on either side of the fifties,

I found some documents in there that didn't belong. So I'd start with the fifties and then go through the others, just in case.

After two hours of fruitless searching, I had found one small newspaper article that mentioned the victim's name and that the authorities were following several leads. Not much to go on. Bingo stirred at my feet, Rocky the cat jumped into my lap, and I sniffled but didn't sneeze. Feeling frustrated, I realized it was time to stretch my legs. I put Rocky down and then petted Bingo before the two of them started roughhousing and chasing each other around the big room.

Walking down the stairs and wondering where the information for the murder could be, I stood in front of the murder exhibit. Something made me reach out and touch the little dent in the plastic—I mean Lexan. For some reason, that dent made me want to solve the murder even more. That poor old woman! As I pondered that, the sound of the back door opening made me shiver. Was it the back door or was it the exhibit that made me shiver?

CHAPTER SIX

BINGO, WHO HAD followed me downstairs, yipped his *I'm happy* bark and ran toward the back door. That, and the sound of Aiden's Van's tennis shoes running toward me, made the shiver evaporate. Instead of waiting for him to reach me, I turned toward the sound of the footfalls and opened my arms, and Aiden jumped into them. I swung him around, snuggling my face into him, and said, "I love you! I love you! I love you!"

Aiden tried to squirm out of my arms, but I held him tight. "Mommy! Mommy! Let me go! I *know* you love me! Mrs. Reilly told me about the mistake, and I get it. I know you love me, and I appreciate that you want to make sure I know now that it's over, but I want to see where the murder was! Please! Set me down!"

I kissed him on his cheek, set him down, and just like that the trauma was over. And yes, that is how my seven-year-old son talks. He reads at an adult level, has a vocabulary better than mine, and except for minor indiscretions, behaves perfectly. And since Mrs. Reilly—that's Pamela, the principal—told him, instead of me and Billy struggling to come up with something appropriate to say, that was a good thing. Did she step outside her bounds to do such a thing? Absolutely not. I appreciated it very much. Pamela knew I was a "new, first-time mother" and that I was a little insecure about it. I was grateful to her for stepping in.

Pamela and I had a special relationship because of how we got acquainted. I had discovered—quite by accident—that Aiden could read. He had been in remedial reading classes, while they tried to get him to read "I hop, you hop, we all hop together." It was so beneath his reading level that he refused to read it. When he tried to get books more to his liking at the school library, the librarian thought he was choosing books for his foster brothers and sisters and told him to let them get their own books.

When I discovered the truth, I marched his cute, little butt and my big butt, over to the school to complain to the principal—Pamela Reilly. She was so appreciative that I had discovered this after the poor kid had been in remedial reading for nearly a year, that she felt like she was in my debt. Aiden did have a hand in the deception since he pretended that he couldn't read, due to his foster brother telling him that he'd get in trouble if they knew he could read so well. But it worked out, and Pamela was so elated that I stood in as advocate for Aiden when I hardly knew him—I had only met him twice—that she recommended to the authorities that they remove Aiden from his current foster situation and ask if I would consider being a foster parent for Aiden.

And I immediately said absolutely not! It hadn't taken me long to fall under Aiden's spell, and I wanted to be a *real* parent to him, not a foster parent. And that's how I came to adopt him; although the adoption wasn't final yet.

"Mommy, Mommy! Yippee! The outline is still here! And the fingerprint powder!" He jumped back into my arms and then squirmed back out of them.

Oh, no! I had been so distracted by trying to find out information about the old murder that I had completely overlooked both the outline of the dead body and the fingerprint powder all over everything. But, my neglect was Aiden's gain. Finally! It made me feel a little better about my neglect.

"Mommy! Mommy! Can I clean it up? Please? Please can I clean it?" He stopped jumping up and down momentarily, the smile faded, and he asked, "Is it okay with Sheriff Billy if we clean it up?"

Leaning down, I scooped him up again and swung him around. "It's okay, and *you* can do it!"

"Yippee! Put me down quick so I can start!"

Kissing him again on the cheek, I put him down, and he rushed off to get the cleaning supplies. I made my way back upstairs to tackle the *Police Beat* files. "C'mon, Bingo. We're not needed here." Bingo followed me up the stairs.

Thirty-five minutes later, I had come up empty on the files, and still had a third of it to go through. Maybe the murder info was in the wrong year. I'd found plenty of misfiled files when I was doing the scanning. I sighed and determined to finish the one I was on first.

Then I heard Aiden's feet trudging up the stairs, and I do mean trudging. Usually, he took two stairs at a time—no matter how many times I discouraged that—and was up here before I realized he had started. He came to the top step and jumped up onto the second floor with both feet. "Mommy?"

I turned toward him. "Yes, sweetie?"

"This isn't as much fun as I thought it'd be. Cleaning up crime scenes is not what it's cracked up to be and *definitely* not something I want to do when I grow up!"

Stifling my laughter, I said, "You don't have to finish, sweetie. I can take care of it." Cracked up to be? Where does he get this stuff?

Aiden sighed. "No, I said I'd do it, and I'll do it. But it's not much fun." He turned to go back downstairs. Aiden was a very conscientious kid.

"Wait!"

He looked at me expectantly. "Yes, Mommy?"

"How about if you take a break from the clean-up work and help me up here?"

His eyes brightened. "Yeah! What can I do?"

"I've been searching all day for the newspaper articles and whatnot on the old murder. Do you happen to know where it might be?"

"Are you looking so you can tie the two murders together? You know, the old one and the new one?"

"Great minds think alike!" I said. "That's exactly what I'm trying to do! But I can't find anything."

"Where are you looking?" he asked.

I held up the *Police Beat* binder that I had been looking through. "This. Police Beat."

"That's the problem, Mommy! I know exactly where it is!" And he skipped off, disappearing into the shelves where the binders were.

A minute later he returned with a binder clutched to his chest. "Here, Mommy. It's in this one."

I took the binder from him. The label on it said *Motor Vehicles/Names*. Oh, great, there already was one labeled *Automobiles*, now I'd have to cross-reference even more. "This one? I don't get it."

Aiden looked at me with his hands on his hips. "Open it, Mommy! It's exactly what you're looking for! I saw it *before*."

By *before*, he meant before he and I were together. When he couldn't read at school, he'd come in here pretending to look at the pictures, but in actuality he'd be reading. This must have been one of the binders he had read back then. When I opened it and leafed through it, there, right in front of me, and to my amazement, was a section labeled *Murders*. "Did you read it already, then?"

"Yeah! That's what gave me the idea to put up the murder exhibit. It's an interesting case. But this new murder makes it even more interesting, don't you think?"

The way he said this made me cock my head and look at him while narrowing my eyes. "Ai-den." I drew it out to emphasize the two syllables. "You're not going to poke your cute little nose into this murder, are you?"

With a deliberately innocent look on his face, he said, "You mean *murders*, right?"

"Aiden! I'm telling you right now that I want you to stay out of this!"

"But, Mommy," he said while taking my hand and looking into my eyes. His blue eyes surrounded by long lashes were enough to charm anybody. "I thought we'd work on it together." He nodded his head. "You 'n' me."

"No, Aiden. I'm serious. This is dangerous business, and I want you to stay out of it. Now why don't you go back downstairs and finish the cleaning."

31

It wasn't a question. It was a statement, to which he responded by lowering his head, nodding once, and retreating down the stairs. I sat there a minute listening for what he was going to do. In no time, I heard him working down there and whistling while he was at it. Aiden was a great kid, with a great attitude. I was so lucky to have him.

And once I knew he was safely ensconced in his work, I returned to the binder. Leafing from one end of the *Murder* section to the other, I realized there was only one murder in it. The Edward Pennington murder.

CHAPTER SEVEN

INSTEAD OF SKIMMING like I usually did, I read every word of every page. It was fascinating reading, with not only the murder, but accusations, betrayal, and suicide. I was just past the middle and totally engulfed in my reading, when I heard Aiden downstairs.

"Sheriff Billy!" And then the thump that signified his jumping into Billy's arms.

Bingo, who had been resting comfortably at my feet, ran down the stairs to greet Billy, too. Although I felt like I should hurry down the stairs and greet him in the manner to which he had grown accustomed—especially since I had treated him so badly the last week or so—I couldn't stop reading the file. So I took a second to say, "Hi, Billy!" and resumed my reading.

So engrossed in the murder and the disparate opinions on the outcome of the case, I didn't know if it was two hours or two minutes later when Billy, followed by Aiden, walked up the stairs. It wasn't until Billy put his hand on my shoulder and gave it a shake that I even realized he and Aiden were standing beside me.

"Lorry? Are you okay? We've been calling you from downstairs. What's going on?"

"You okay, Mommy?" Aiden asked, concerned, now standing on the other side of me.

I looked up, almost dazed, having a difficult time reconciling the present from the past. "Oh, yeah, sorry. This stuff is incredible!" Slipping a plastic ruler into the file to mark my place, I closed the binder and looked up at Billy.

"So Aiden tells me that Pamela explained what had happened, so I guess we don't have to do that now."

"Yeah, Mommy was just being silly. But she's back to normal now. She even gave me a five minute hug!"

In an exaggerated sad voice, Billy said, "How come *I* didn't get a five minute hug?" He took my hand, pulled me up in front of him, and wrapped his arms around me.

Aiden said, "It wasn't really five minutes, Sheriff Billy, it just felt like that."

Then, from the side, Aiden wrapped his arms around me, so it was a whole family hug. Aiden would have gone from the back, but with my big butt, he would have been too far away. Bingo jumped up on my leg to make the hug complete, and even Rocky the cat jumped on the chair and rubbed against us.

Aiden stepped away, Rocky jumped down, and I felt Billy sigh in my arms before he pulled out of the hug. "Well," he said, "it wasn't quite five minutes, but it was a good start!" Then he kissed me on the lips, gave me one more squeeze, and backed away. "You ready to go?"

Looking down at the binder on my desk regretfully, I checked my watch. "It's still early. How 'bout if I meet you there?" I looked at Billy hopefully.

"Oh, come on, Mom! You can read it later! Let's go to Grammy and Grampy's!"

Martha and Hugo weren't really Aiden's grandparents, but when we lived with them in their bed and breakfast before we got our house, the three of them became so close, that they became Grammy and Grampy with everybody's mutual consent.

Billy smiled an understanding smile at me—he knew me so well—and pulled Aiden to him. "Hey, little pard, why don't you ride with me over there, and your Mommy can drive herself in a few minutes? Is that okay with you?"

In answer, Aiden jumped up and down twice, shouted, "Shotgun!" and ran down the stairs.

I put my arms around Billy's neck. "Thank you, Sheriff Billy. I love you."

He kissed me, unwrapped my arms, and looked at his watch. "You have fifteen minutes to read and five minutes to drive over there. Okay? I'll see you at five-thirty." Then he kissed me again and walked down the stairs.

I stepped to the top of the stairs and called after him, "It only takes two minutes to drive there, so I can read for eighteen minutes!"

Billy chuckled, shook his head, and continued down the stairs. I could hear Aiden at the back door yelling to Billy to hurry up. Picking up the binder again, I found my place, and started reading before my butt hit the chair.

"Lorry! Lorry! Do I have to come up there and slap your face to get your attention? Lorry!" Petra called out from the bottom of the stairs.

35

I was on the final page of the murder debacle or she probably would have had to come upstairs. Petra wouldn't really have slapped me, and she wasn't really being disrespectful. Sometimes I needed an extra *push* to listen, and the *slapping your face* gambit was what she chose.

"Yeah, Petra. What's up?"

"Billy just called my *cell phone*"—she emphasized that because we don't answer the business phone after five —"to say you're late for the party!"

"It's not a party, Petra, just dinner at Martha's to talk about the wedding."

"Whatever, Lorry! Get down here and get over there! You're late! My duty is done; I'm going back to studying now. Bye."

I looked at my watch. Uh oh. Five-thirty-five. It was late. But instead of closing the binder and walking downstairs, I *had to* finish reading the final page. I knew Martha and Hugo would understand—the question was, would Billy? No matter, I had to finish the final page. I'm a slow reader, but it wouldn't take long.

When I finished the murder *story*, I closed the binder, feeling satisfied. And then I looked at my watch. Oh, no! It was five-forty-five. Rushing down the stairs as fast as I could in my heels, which was not all that fast because I didn't want to fall topsy-turvy down the stairs, I yelled "Goodbye" to Petra, and slipped out the back door.

CHAPTER EIGHT

ON MY RUSH over to Martha and Hugo's place, careful not to exceed the speed limit and thus get a ticket —it wouldn't look good for that to happen to the sheriff's intended—I forgot about what I had just read. It was interesting, but right now I was holding up people whom I loved from eating dinner. Some things are more important than other things. And I was halfway there before I realized that Bingo wasn't with me. I hoped that he had gone with Billy and Aiden.

Turning on Meadowside Lane, I pulled into the driveway of Martha and Hugo's house. They called it Martha's Bed and Breakfast although Hugo ran it while Martha was at work. The tall blue and gray Victorian was a gorgeous house with one of those towers rising from the upper floor. When I lived here, and still when I visit, I always imagined Rapunzel up there letting down her long, blond hair. But there was no Rapunzel today. There was only Billy standing on the Goldstein's porch with his hands on his hips and looking angry. There was some consolation in Bingo wagging his tail and sitting at Billy's heels.

Billy doesn't get angry at me often—and heaven knows he has a right to with all my antics—but he sure looked ticked off this time. I guess it was because I had put him off for the last week about the wedding, and now that we were finally going to talk about it, I turn up late. He was usually understanding, but I guess I had pushed him past the tipping point this time.

I stepped out of the car, smiling what I hoped was a beguiling smile, and shrugged. He pointed to his watch and scowled. Bingo ran over and jumped up on me; I leaned over to pat him without taking my eyes off Billy. As I approached him, his expression didn't change, and just when I thought he was going to open his mouth and scold me, Hugo came through the door and burst into song as he often does.

"Here she is now, so late late late. And that made us have to wait wait wait. But I guess that was just our fate fate fate!" He held the door open for us with a flourish. "Come on, Lorry! You're worth waiting for! Isn't she, Sheriff Billy?" Hugo normally didn't call Billy *Sheriff Billy*, but I think he was trying to make a point. What it was, I wasn't sure.

Billy followed me into the house, and then Hugo closed the door and hurried past us. He usually did the cooking, and he even still had his apron on. I thought maybe Billy would swat my behind or something, but instead he walked close behind me, put his hands on my shoulders, and whispered in my ear, "I'm mad at you for this, Lorry, but I'm still madly in love with you, so I'll let it go."

How could anyone not love a man like that? I turned around, gave him a hug, and then Aiden ran in grabbing my hand. "Mommy! Mommy!" he scolded. "You're very late! Come on, I'm hungry!" And he let my hand go and scuttled off into the kitchen.

When Billy and I walked through the kitchen door, Martha pulled me aside to the far edge of the kitchen. She whispered, "Does Aiden like spaghetti squash?"

"No, he hates it."

"Then don't tell him it's in this recipe. It's called Spaghetti Squash Pie, and you'll love it!"

I hoped so, because I wasn't a fan of spaghetti squash, either. But I smiled and nodded and joined Billy and Aiden at the table. After Martha and Hugo had put everything on the table, we all started eating. Besides the big casserole dish full of Spaghetti Squash Pie, there was a plate of asparagus, which Aiden and I loved, and salad. And it smelled like there was something cooking in the oven, but it was too early to tell what it was. I thought that was strange, because of Hugo's diet after his heart attack, but then Martha explained.

"Okay, everybody, I have an announcement to make. Hugo went to the doctor a few weeks ago, and since the doctor was unhappy with Hugo's loss of weight progress, he put Hugo on a new diet. It's called keto, and it will help him lose weight, and keep his heart healthy while it happens."

Hugo stood up, pulled off his apron and faced sideways so we could see his belly. There was hardly anything there. "See?" he said. "It works!"

"Yes, it does work! Hugo has already lost twenty more pounds, and it's only been a few weeks. And the food has been great! He doesn't feel deprived at all. So anyway, this is one of the recipes, it's called"—she shot a warning glance at Hugo, but he wasn't paying attention —"Spaghetti Pie, and it's one of our favorites! Enjoy!"

Hugo said, "I thought it was called—"

Martha nodded as she interrupted him. "Yes, Hugo, it's called Spaghetti Pie, like I said."

"Oh," he said sheepishly and returned to his plate of food.

When I finished my salad, I took a deep breath and bit into a forkful of spaghetti pie. And another. And another. It was delicious! "Martha, this is fantastic!" I turned to Aiden who also seemed to be enjoying it. "Aiden? Do you like it?"

"It's mmmm mmmm good, Mommy! Get the recipe!"

Billy liked everything, so I didn't even question him. "Martha, could I get the recipe from you?"

"Certainly, my dear." She winked at me. "So I heard there was another murder at the historical society today. What now?"

Hugo chuckled and choked on his mouthful. We all looked at him to make sure he was okay. When he swallowed, he sang out, "Another murder, dark and gory, follows around our little Lorry. So if you don't want to turn up dead, we best be talking about her getting wed!"

"Thank you, Hugo. It is about time for that," said Billy "But I'll say that it was an old woman, and I expect to get a lead or two tomorrow morning. Nick tracked down the people who were in there just before the shooting. Two of them came in today. One said they saw a man go into the back part of the exhibit area, and one said it was a woman. It's one to one, so far. We'll see what tomorrow brings. Now let's talk wedding!"

But the damage had been done. I had stopped thinking about it on my rush over to dinner, but now that Martha brought it up again, the vision of the old woman on the floor, and everything I had read that afternoon, kept playing in front of my eyes. I couldn't seem to think of anything else. The conversation went on around me, but I wasn't involved in it. I couldn't be with all those visions in front of me.

"Lorry? What do you think of that idea? Lorry?"

Billy put his hand on my arm and gave it a gentle shake. "Lorry? *Where* are you?"

I shook my head to try to clear it, but it didn't work. "The murder," I said. "I can't get it out of my mind. That's why I was late, too. Everything I read today about the murder in the fifties—it was an incredibly interesting story."

Billy's voice deepened and had an edge to it. "More interesting than our wedding?"

"Maybe we should talk about the wedding after dinner, then?" asked Martha, trying to turn the conversation into a friendlier direction. She was always the mediator. "Why don't you tell us the story about the murder, Lorry?"

"Ha!" said Aiden. "Story, Lorry. It rhymes."

Billy frowned but nodded his head.

And I put down my fork, swallowed the spaghetti pie that I had been chewing, and told them the story of the murder of Edward R. Pennington.

CHAPTER NINE

THE ELDEST OF three siblings, Edward R. Pennington was in the prime of life. He had attended college, had worked his way up in his father's firm, and was about to take over the company. His father, Erwin Pennington, wanted to retire so he could care for his invalid wife, Esther. The middle sibling was Evelyn, who was married to an ambitious young attorney, Howard Strong. The youngest sibling, Everett, had married young, just out of high school, and was an auto mechanic. He and his wife, Dorothy, had a five-year-old daughter named Virginia.

"Virginia Pennington?" asked Aiden. "That's the name of the dead woman." Everyone looked at Aiden, and he shrugged. "The Internet," he said.

Everybody turned to look at me. I nodded to indicate he was correct. Billy said, "Hush, Aiden. Let your mother tell the story."

On the afternoon of the murder, like every other Thursday, Everett was at the library studying to become a master mechanic. But he always sat upstairs by himself, where it was quiet, and left via an outside staircase. So besides confirming that he had come in at one o'clock, no one could give him an alibi.

The murder occurred in Rutledge at the family home where Edward lived with his parents. It was a not very modest home right here on Meadowside Lane. In case you're wondering, it has since been torn down and another house rebuilt on the lot. The father found Edward on the living room floor with a shot in the chest.

The murder weapon, a specially made pearl-handled Colt Python revolver, was found at the scene. Both men, Edward and Everett, had received matching guns the previous Christmas from their parents. Edward's was still at the house in his room. Everett's was missing. In addition, ballistic tests proved that the weapon left at the scene was the gun that murdered Edward. It had Everett's very smeared fingerprints on it. Another piece of evidence was a cigar butt a couple of feet from the gun. It was Everett's brand, El Producto. His father also smoked cigars, but he smoked a Swiss brand, Rössli.

So, Everett: no alibi, his gun, his fingerprints, and his cigar butt, all found at the scene. Were there any other suspects to the murder? Yes, but no one of consequence. His sister Evelyn, who had claimed to be shopping in West Rutledge—which we all know is currently named Coyote Moon—had no alibi and certainly knew where Edward kept his gun, but as she had no access to Everett's gun, they eliminated her. There was a teenager, Dale James, who had stolen from the family and was working as a gardener to repay his debt. He worked on the day of the murder and disappeared before they could question him. No one actually thought he did it, though, because nothing was missing from the house. Dale

James. The name sound familiar? It's Zack's grandfather, who returned to town after everything was settled.

A dentist was also suspected, since he and Edward had a feud going about some dental work. But he had a solid alibi: he was drilling out a cavity when the murder occurred.

The other unlikely suspect, besides the dentist, was the doctor who had given Edward's mother, Esther Pennington, an incorrect prescription which had caused some of her health issues. It was too high of a dose of pain killer for her headaches that caused her to fall down and break her hip. At the time of the murder, she was in a convalescent home in West Rutledge. There was a pending court case against the doctor, and plenty of bitterness against all involved. But he, too, had a solid alibi. He was between patients, but from the last time he was seen to the next time he was seen gave him no time to have driven to the Pennington house and committed the murder.

Everything pointed to Everett, including something that had happened a week previous to the killing. Someone had cut Edward's brake lines. It was only a small cut, and the outcome had been a small fender-bender on his way home from work. But naturally it made Everett, the mechanic, the natural suspect.

When the authorities questioned Everett, he mentioned how everything pointed directly to him, and he wondered why anyone would be so stupid as to leave the murder weapon *with fingerprints* right at the scene, as well as the cigar butt. He claimed it was a setup.

The police said a clever criminal would do just that and say it was a frame. According to the newspaper article, the police told Everett, and I quote, "We've got you dead to rights, and you'll be going away for a long time. Or maybe not so long if you get the death penalty." He was released because of his father's influence in town, because he never thought one of his sons could kill another.

What happened next was tragic. Everett's wife, Dorothy, was pregnant with their second child. When she read the account in the newspaper about the death penalty, she got so upset that she went into labor several months too early and lost the child, a little boy. Everett blamed himself for causing the death of his son, and he went directly to the family home, retrieved Edward's gun, and shot himself.

The father, Erwin, still needed to retire so he could care for his wife. So, his daughter's husband, the attorney Howard Strong, was drafted into the position of president of the company, and since his wife, Evelyn, was the only heir, the two of them inherited the business and the family fortune.

The story finished, I shrugged my shoulders, and said, "And I think that's a pretty big incentive for murder and a frame job. I'd like to know what Evelyn was *really* doing when she claimed to be shopping."

CHAPTER TEN

"SHE WAS PROBABLY just shopping," said Billy. "You make too much of this stuff, Lorry."

"Didn't you say one of your witnesses said they saw a woman go into the back? Maybe it was the daughter, Jacqueline, or maybe it was Evelyn. Nobody would have paid her any attention. She'd be older than the dead woman by now."

"The daughter was sick in the bathroom all morning, Lorry. Kasey confirmed that," said Billy. Kasey Brannigan was my cousin who worked next door in the Koffee Korner Kafe. *Next door* being relative, because it was part of the same building.

"Billy, you know how busy the cafe is at that time in the morning. Do you really think Kasey would even *notice* if the woman left and returned?"

Martha stood up. "How about dessert? We are supposed to be talking about your wedding, not having the two of you argue over a murder! Who's interested in chocolate cheesecake pie?"

Aiden raised his hand. "Me! Me! I love pie!"

46

Martha and I cleared the table while Hugo served the pie. I sat down and took one bite expecting some horrible diet dessert, and what a surprise I got. "Martha, this is delicious!"

"Tell Hugo. He made it."

"Hugo, this is wonderful. I can't believe something this good is on your diet!"

"Keto diet," said Hugo. "Nothing like it. We bought an ice cream maker, and you should taste some of the ice cream recipes we have! Deee-licious!"

After that, the only sounds in the room were those of appreciative mmmm mmmm noises and forks scraping plates. Their kitchen had off-white wallpaper with etched red velvet flowers. It was tasteful and beautiful. We sat at an octagonal wormwood dining table—which I suppose was fine if you were into worms, which I was not.

It felt good to sit around with everyone and have a group discussion. With everyone so engrossed in their dessert, it gave me a chance to look around the room at the people I shared this dessert with. Martha was dressed in a stunning yellow pantsuit. I couldn't see the pants now, but I had noticed them when she was standing at the sink. They were solid yellow, and the blouse was flowered to match. I bet she had on a blazer when she was at work today. Hugo had his famous red *Too many cooks and all that nonsense* apron on over a dark blue sweatsuit—his usual garb.

Billy was still in his work clothes which consisted of dark brown slacks and a light brown shirt. He always wore a bolo tie with it, and today's had a buffalo with a turquoise eye. He had probably left his signature Smokey Bear hat in the car, because it wasn't with him. And sweet little Aiden wore his usual blue jeans, his Van's tennis shoes, and a new red sweatshirt that had a picture of a unicorn on it with *Unicorn Whisperer* written in rainbow letters. I thought it was a little girlish for him, but he wanted it, so I bought it for him. I never had any doubts about Aiden's sexuality, because he was all boy. But if he did turn out to be gay, I would love him just as much anyway, because he was mine.

When we finished, Aiden said, "Grampy, can Mommy have that recipe, too?" And we all laughed.

"All right," said Billy, a little crossly, "can we please talk about the wedding *now*?" The way he said it struck the rest of us funny, and we all laughed bordering on hysteria. "What?" he asked. "What's so funny?"

I patted his hand. "Nothing, darling. Let's talk about our wedding." I kissed him on his muscled arm.

"Where would you would like to get married?" asked Martha. "I know there's that beautiful little chapel in Sedona. How about there?"

Neither Billy nor I was Catholic, and I was pretty sure that chapel was a Catholic church, but who was I to argue. "That sounds reasonable," I said, noncommittally. "Billy?"

Billy sighed. "Honestly, I just want to get married. I don't care where." And that comment sent us all into hysteria again.

I patted his hand again. "It's all right, honey. We can get married wherever you want to. Honest. Anywhere you want."

"Oh, that chapel is so beautiful," said Martha. "You will make such a lovely bride, Lorry." She looked off into the distance like she was imagining me in my white wedding dress. "Have you decided who will be your maid of honor?"

"Petra thinks it should be her, and with Sam back in town, she's in the running. After what happened before Thanksgiving, I don't even know if Kasey will attend, so it's undecided for now. But I'm thinking to make matters simple, it should be you, Martha. Then no one will be upset."

"So I guess that makes me the *best man*, then," said Hugo. He puffed up his chest and lifted his head to the sky. "I always knew I was the *best* man."

"Oh, Hugo. You're going to give the bride away. Right, Lorry?"

"Absolutely. No doubt about that. It's everything else that we're undecided about."

"Okay. Let's leave that for now. Do you know how soon you want to get married?"

"Would tonight be too soon?" asked Billy, sending us all into laughter again. This time, though, Billy joined us. "I spent the last week wondering if the wedding was even going to happen, so really, I'd like to do it soon, before my bride-to-be changes her mind."

"I *never* changed my mind. And I *won't* change my mind. I couldn't think of a thing you could do that would make me change my mind." Then I thought about that scoundrel, Eddie, who I used to be married to, so I added, "Well, maybe there is a thing or two, but you're not that kind of guy."

Billy looked at me and blinked, but said nothing. Then Martha spoke up again. "Okay, so we know that we want it soon, and you don't much care where. How about if we all go to Sedona this weekend and take a look at the chapel? Maybe we can arrange everything right then."

"That would be awesome." He looked at me. "Hon, is that okay with you?"

49

"Sure, Billy. Sedona this weekend. I'll be there!"

"Mommy," said Aiden. "Can't we all go together?"

"Mommy was just kidding, Aiden. That's what we'll do. We'll all go together."

Billy stood up. "All right, it's settled then. We're getting married as soon as possible and going to Sedona this weekend to check out a chapel. Perfect!" He smiled at Martha and Hugo. "Thank you both for a delicious dinner and dessert. It was scrumptious! We'll see you this weekend."

Aiden and I stood up, said our thank yous and goodbyes, and walked outside with Billy. Martha and Hugo followed us out and waved as we walked toward our vehicles. Hugo called out, "Now that we have all been fed, Lorry and Billy are about to be wed. They'll get married as soon as can be; and soon will be an old couple like Martha and me!"

Martha said, "Oh, Hugo." And he hugged her.

Aiden walked between us, and Billy said, "Aiden, why don't you get in Mommy's car. I need to talk to her alone for just a minute."

"I know, I know," said Aiden. "Little pitchers have big ears."

"I've never said that to you, Aiden!" I said, and Billy agreed.

Aiden laughed. "I know. But I used to hear it all the time at the foster place." That's what he called the foster home he used to live in, *the foster place.* Being one of ten kids, there wasn't a lot of time for any of them. "See ya in a minute."

Billy waited until Martha and Hugo turned out the light and then pulled me to him. "I'm sorry if I acted petulant tonight. It was just that I had more than a week of worrying whether you were going to marry me or not. And today, after I found out that everything was okay, it affected me more than I thought it would." He kissed me. "I didn't want to lose you, Lorry, and I was so afraid that I would."

"I'm so sorry, Billy. Let's get married right away."

"Let's hope the chapel has an opening real soon."

CHAPTER ELEVEN

BILLY SAID HE still had work to do on the murder case, so he didn't come over to my house like he usually did. So Aiden and I went home and spent the rest of the evening—there wasn't much left of it—reading, as *we* usually did. My family was a long line of readers. I would have to say that my family read like other families drink.

I remember a story that my grandmother used to tell. She was the third child in a family of eight, and it was her responsibility to take care of the babies. So she'd sit beside the rocker and rock the baby, except that she would also have a book in her hands, reading. When the story got exciting, she would sometimes rock the cradle too much and the baby would cry, but she didn't hear it because she was so engrossed in the book. The same thing happened when the going was slow, and she forgot to rock the cradle. As she related the story, she got yelled at about that more than a few times.

And my grandfather was also a big reader. He had immigrated here from *the old country*, as he called it, and spoke seven languages. So when he was reading, you never knew what language he would be reading in. What I remember best is him sitting in the only bathroom in the house, reading away, while everyone else was knocking on the door for him to get out so they could use the toilet.

I looked at my watch and announced that we should finish our respective chapters. Sometimes Aiden would sneak in a second chapter, because he was a faster reader than I was. But tonight, I finished first and went into the other room to get into my nightgown. Aiden followed a few minutes later and slipped into his jammies. Then our routine dictated that I go into his room, and we would take turns reading. Tonight was my night, and we were in the middle of *Anne of Green Gables*. He had heard from his teacher that it was a classic, so he wanted to read it. Although I had to admit that I didn't appreciate all his choices, with this book, I liked it, too.

The following morning, I had a couple of soft boiled eggs, and Aiden had cereal and juice. I volunteered to make him anything he wanted, but cereal was always his choice. Except of course, pancakes. He always wanted pancakes, but I reserved those for Sundays only.

In less than an hour, we were ready to leave for school and work. Aiden wore his usual jeans and Van's tennis shoes. And he topped that off with a light blue sweatshirt with a picture of a kid hugging a tree. It said, *Trees are for hugging*.

I wore a black and white checked skirt—the big kind of checks, two inches across, and a white blouse with a modest black design down the front where the buttons were. And of course my versatile black heels. I may be a full-figured woman, but I was a *well-dressed* full-figured woman. And Bingo wore his black collar.

The three of us entered the car, I drove to the historical society, parked in the back, and then Bingo and I walked Aiden to school. Returning to work, I said good morning to Petra, checked my email on the downstairs computer, got a pen and paper from my desk, and walked to the murder exhibit.

The top of it said *Who Killed Edward?* and had an eight by ten picture of him on the left hand side. To the right of that were pictures of the suspects: Everett, the doctor, the dentist, and the missing teen-aged gardener. As I stared at the suspects, I searched my memory for what the old woman had said. Oh, yes. "You're missing two of the suspects, a man *and* a woman." Okay, the woman has to be the sister Evelyn, whom I also thought was a suspect. But who would the other male suspect be? Thinking back to everything I had read, I couldn't remember any other man who was a suspect. Beside everything on the top of the exhibit, I wrote down my conclusions and questions.

To the left of the picture of the victim, hanging on a hanger on the side wall of the exhibit, was the white shirt of the deceased, with the hole in it surrounded by blood. Aiden insisted that be there, against my better judgment. But nobody objected, so I guess he was right. Beneath the pictures of the suspects was another eight by ten picture—this one horizontal rather than vertical—of a class picture with twelve children in it of different ages. I suspected that both Edward and Everett were in the picture, as well as Evelyn.

Beneath that was a picture of the cigar butt found at the scene. Next to that was a picture of the cut brake line. And next to that was a polygraph printout with a brief explanation of what it meant typed up in big letters next to it. Everett took and passed the lie detector test, but that wouldn't be enough to clear him—not that it mattered anyway, considering what happened.

At the bottom of the exhibit was the murder weapon. The pearl-handled revolver. I squinted my eyes and reached out to touch the nick in the hard plastic—Lexan —door of the exhibit. It might be a good idea to remove that gun, so whoever killed Virginia Pennington and put the nick in the door, wasn't tempted to try again. Why she or he would want it was the big question though. Another thing that the woman had said—or almost said —was that the gun was not the murder weapon.

So if she didn't mean *the gun is not the murder weapon,* then what else could she have meant? The gun is not the murder—murdered man's gun? That makes no sense. And nothing else came to mind. After writing down the rest of the items on exhibit, I wrote down another question. What could she have meant?

And then I realized what it was. It made perfect sense and confirmed my suspicions about the murder. I had it!

CHAPTER TWELVE

I STOOD THERE congratulating myself on figuring the whole thing out. The reason the dead woman said that wasn't the murder weapon is because the sister, whom I had my doubts about from the beginning—shopping indeed!—also had a gun, gifted to her from her father. It made sense. But no one ever thought to ask about that. She shot her older brother, then framed her younger brother for the crime. The motive being exactly what happened: she and her husband obtained the entire Pennington business *and* fortune. It was a simple matter of deduction, and it had to be her.

Walking to Petra's desk, with a spring in my step to tell her how smart I was, I said, "Petra, guess what? I solved the murder!" And then I added, "I solved the murder!" just because I was so proud of myself.

"What now, Lorry?" she turned around with half an eye on her computer studies and a frown for me.

"It was the sister! She had a gun that nobody knew about! She did it and framed her younger brother by leaving *his* gun at the scene of the crime!"

Now she turned all the way around to face me. "Wait a minute. Wasn't there a ballistic test done on the murder weapon and didn't it match?"

My pride crumpled. Petra was right. "Oh, yeah," I said in almost a whisper.

"And didn't you think the murderer was the woman's daughter who was so sick here the day of the murder?"

I felt like I was the Wicked Witch of the West and someone had just thrown water on me. "Right again," I said and slunk away to my desk, as my pride and my glory over solving the murder shrunk away to nothingness.

Petra was right. I was certain the murderer was the woman's daughter. But I was just as certain that Edward's sister was the murderer. Wait! What was I thinking? It wasn't the same murder! I could be right in both instances! Why not?

I straightened up in my chair and began to think everything through. Could the woman, Jacqueline Pennington, have faked the stink in the bathroom? What's that quote? Oh, yeah. *If it stinks like poop, it probably is poop.* Does that answer my question? She certainly stank in there. Does that eliminate her as a suspect? I wasn't ready to make that commitment yet. Aren't there devices in novelty stores that stink like that? Wouldn't that be the perfect alibi?

And the sister. What about her? There was a ballistic test on the gun in question, and it came back positive for the murder weapon? Does that eliminate *her* as a suspect? I wasn't ready to make that commitment yet, either. And while I pondered that puzzle—two murders, two female suspects—I heard the bell on the door jingle, and I turned my head to see who was coming in.

"Sam!" I said as she walked in. She smiled broadly at me, and we hugged. "How are you?"

Sam was wearing blue jeans—granted they were expensive designer labels—and a sweater knitted so it looked tie-dyed. I said *tie-dyed*. This was the woman who shared with me the *Best Dressed in School* award when we were in high school. Both of us being clothes hounds is one of the areas that we had in common. And now she wears *tie-dye*?

"I'm doing great," she said. "I came to see how you're doing with your wedding preparations."

I hadn't seen Sam since just after Thanksgiving when we had lunch together after the *affair* at the school. It was something we both—especially me—would like to forget. But I had told her last time I saw her that Billy had asked me to marry him. "Well, they haven't gone anywhere yet —"

"Oh," she stepped back, reluctant to pry, but obviously wanting to know. "Um, is everything still okay?"

"Yes, yes, we're still getting married and all. We're going to Sedona this weekend to check out the chapel there."

"Do you want to get married in a chapel?" She looked thoughtful for a second and then added, "Isn't that a Catholic church? I don't remember you being Catholic —"

"You're right. I'm not. And I'm not sure if it's Catholic or not, or even if you have to be Catholic to get married there. We'll find all that out this weekend. Billy just wants to get married. He doesn't care where, and I don't either."

"Glad everything is *kind of* on schedule then. How's that boychik of yours?"

"What?"

"Oh, sorry! I've been hanging with Mark's folks so much, and they speak Yiddish, that I've been re-picking up words from them. Boychik is boy. How's Aiden?"

"He's doing great. Cast's off, and he's back in his karate class." Aiden had broken his arm, but it was all healed now. "How's Willow and Sage?" These *pleasantries* bored me. We never used to have to go through all this when we were in high school together. Of course, back then there was only ourselves to worry about. Now, we both had children and a man in our lives. It was a fair trade-off.

"I've been so busy with family and driving back and forth to the valley to see Mark's folks, that I haven't had a chance to do anything else."

"I get that," I said, but Billy's folks were gone and so were mine. There were no folks to drive to see. I wished there were.

"What else have you been doing?" Sam asked. "Oh! I heard about the murder here! That's exciting!"

"I'll tell ya, the more murders there are around here, the less exciting each one becomes! Frankly, I'm tired of it."

"Yeah, she says that," said Petra from the other room, "but she's hot on the trail of the murderer."

"Hush up, Petra!"

"Hush up. From the sixteen hundreds. Meaning to suppress talk for secrecy's sake."

"That's enough, Petra," I said. And then to Sam, "Okay, okay, I'm not sure hot on the trail is the correct description, but I am trying to figure out who killed the old woman *and* who killed the man from sixty-some years ago. But I've run into a stumbling block or two."

"Have you thought about meditating over it?" Sam asked.

I had never known Sam to be too religious. "What?" I asked, not sure I heard right.

"Oh, Lorry!" she said, tapping my arm. "I see how you're looking at me. Oy vey. I don't mean in a religious way, I mean in a, you know, spiritual way."

"Um, oh," I said, nodding my head, but not knowing what she meant.

"You know! Like Buddhists do, or people who practice yoga. You know! Meditating!"

"I think I've lived in un-sophisticated Coyote Moon and now back in Rutledge for too long. I don't know much about meditating."

"Om! Om! You sit silently, quiet your mind, and then repeat one word like *om* or love or peace or something like that, or you focus on your breathing. I do it all the time. It helps me decompress from time with the kids."

"Oh," I said, not really knowing what else to say.

"Hey! That's it! That's the answer! When you go to Sedona, go to one of the vortexes and meditate over the murders. That will bring you clarity! Try it when you go there! Really! It might help." When I just looked at her, she added, "Oh, sorry, Lorry. I gave you the whole megillah when all you wanted was a tiny piece."

I wasn't even sure I wanted a tiny piece, but if something would give me clarity on these murders, I was all for it. "I'll give it some thought, Sam. Thank you."

"No problem! Glad to help. I have to run now. I have to schlep all the way to Coyote Moon to take care of something for Mark. Which makes no sense to me since he works there, but you know how men are! I love him, but, you know! See ya later!"

Nodding again, I smiled at her. She already had me thinking again about the murders. Maybe some clarity would do me some good. "Bye, Sam!" But for now, I wanted to forget about them and get back to work.

CHAPTER THIRTEEN

I WALKED SLOWLY upstairs trying to decipher what Sam had just told me. It was bad enough trying to interpret her Yiddish words, but this new spiritual stuff of hers was even worse. Although I knew I could use the clarity, I had no idea what a vortex was or where to even begin searching for one. Sitting at my desk, I left the *Children* binder leaning up against the wall and returned to the binder with the murder documents in it. I could work while satisfying my inquisitive crime-solving nature.

And I wouldn't feel guilty even if I did no work at all. When I first came to work here, I was desperate for a job and living in a roach motel just on the other side of the Rutledge River. But shortly after I started, I found out that my mother's money—and there was a lot—was not given to charity when she died as I was told, but it was little by little *available* to me. A few months after that, when a certain *incident* occurred in my life, the bulk of my mother's fortune was given to me. And when I say bulk, I mean bulk that was bigger than me, if you could imagine such a thing. I could spend frivolously for the rest of my life and not make a dent in it.

But where I'm going with this is that after I inherited the fortune, I told Martha that I would work for free. And she told me that because of insurance reasons, that wasn't possible. So I volunteered to work for minimum wage, and whenever I received my paycheck, I donated the whole thing back to the historical society. It's worked out very well for me. I have something to do—besides playing golf at the country club, which I detest—and they get a good worker. Well, good in that I'm responsible and reliable, and when I'm working, I'm working hard. But, as you've heard, I'm not always working. Sometimes I just do my own thing.

I'm not doing it behind Martha's back. I discussed the matter with her, because I didn't want to take the chance of feeling guilty about it. And she said that since I wasn't actually getting paid, and I was getting some work done, it was fine. It's more like most of the work done—at least most of the time. It's not every day that I find a dead body and need to solve the murder—it's more like every other day. Or something.

So I returned to the *Murder* binder—well, it was the *Motor Vehicle/Names* binder—but we're among friends here, so I'll call it the murder binder. We're friends, right?

I began reading the documents again and then scanning them. Now that I wasn't in such a hurry, maybe I could glean another fact or two from them. Maybe they would give me enough clarity so I wouldn't have to figure out what a vortex was. With Bingo at my feet, I settled down to get some work done, hoping to discover something I had missed before.

Several hours of scanning and cross-referencing later, I had found nary a new fact or clue. Disappointed, I leaned over to pet Bingo, and when he wasn't there, I remembered that he had left some time ago to spend time with Rocky. Then I heard Aiden come running up the stairs. Bingo suddenly appeared and stood at the top whining and wagging his tail so hard he almost fell over.

"Hi, Bingo!" Aiden leaned down to hug and kiss Bingo and then proceeded to me. Sloppy seconds. I hate that. "Hi, Mommy! Can we work together on the murder now?"

Hugging him, I said, "Sorry, sweetie, I think we have to let the murder go now and let Daddy solve it." Billy wasn't technically Daddy yet until we married, but it was close enough that I could say that. Besides, Aiden knew what I meant.

"Oh, Mommy." I could feel his arm extend to the binder I was working on. "But you're still reading about the murder!"

"I'm scanning it. Doing my job. And I was just about to put it away, anyway." I put a placeholder into the murder binder, set it aside, and picked up the *Children* binder. "See? All done for now."

He pulled out of my arms clearly disappointed. "Oh, Mommy. I was hoping we could go through the other evidence together."

"Sorry, baby. You need to read or work on your coloring book. Go on, scoot! I need to get back to work."

"All right. I'll go." He hopped down the stairs one step at a time with a big pause in between, probably hoping that I'd change my mind. He was so adult most of the time, but hopping down the stairs? It was good though. I needed the reminder he was just seven, no matter how adult he sometimes acted.

The rest of the afternoon sped by. Aiden and Bingo and I drove home, had dinner and watched a documentary on animal migration with Billy, and then he left and we got ready for bed. After tucking Aiden in for the night, I lay in bed, cuddled up with Bingo, and thought how good it felt to let the murder go and not think about it. That was before I knew what was coming in the morning.

CHAPTER FOURTEEN

THE NEXT MORNING was our usual routine until the three of us stepped outside to leave. It had started snowing, and there was a light dusting on the ground. Big wet flakes fell from the sky. Snow in Arizona is fickle. One minute it will be snowing, and the next minute it will have turned to rain. The sky overhead was still dark, but I expected it to warm up as the day progressed, so this snow was probably short lived.

When Aiden saw it, he ran out to the lawn trying unsuccessfully to make a snowball. There was hardly any snow there, and when he picked it up, it melted in his hand. He looked at me sadly as Bingo ran circles around him snapping his jaws at the falling flakes. That made both Aiden and me laugh as we got into the car. Bingo jumped into the back seat with Aiden.

"Oh, Bingo! Your feet are wet!" said Aiden.

"Tell him to get on the floor, Aiden," I said from the front seat. Aiden usually let Bingo get away with too much, so I wanted Aiden to be the one to tell him, so Bingo would get used to listening to him.

"Bingo, down!"

"Aiden, down is when you want him to lie down."

"But I want him to lie down on the floor."

"Well, what did he do when you told him 'down'?"

"He laid down next to me." Aiden sighed and said, "Bingo, off! Get on the floor."

In the rearview mirror, I saw Aiden's arm move, and I presumed that it was toward the floor. And since I heard nothing else from the back seat, I figured Bingo had done what he was told. "Good job, Aiden." A minute later, it was still snowing, and I had to ask Aiden another question, although I knew him well enough to know the answer. "Would you like me to drop you off at school so you don't get wet?"

"No! I want to walk to school in the snow!"

"There's not much of it, and it's pretty wet," I said, hoping he'd see my point of view.

"Snow is snow, Mommy. And I want to walk in the snow!"

I parked, and then Aiden and I argued about Bingo walking with us or staying in the car. Aiden wanted him, and there was no way I would allow that again. The last time it happened, I had to smell wet dog all morning. Bingo wasn't happy about it, either, because even Rocky ignored him until he dried off. So, if you're wondering who won the argument, I did. Aiden and I walked to school by ourselves. I pulled my hood over my head, and Aiden hopped most of the way there, with his head to the sky and his mouth open.

"I *love* the snow!" he announced as we walked up the path to the school's front door. "Not as much as I love you, though, Mommy!" He kissed me and disappeared into the school.

I hurried back to the historical society, got Bingo out of the car with a minimum of wetness involved, and entered through the back door. "Hello, Petra," I said as I walked past her desk. She made an unintelligible sound and kept studying. After turning on the computer, I sat at my desk and tried to get warm. The snow had blown under my hood, and my head was wet. And curly. But my head was always curly, so nothing had changed. But wet and curly is a whole different story than dry and curly. I'm not sure why, but it's true. It's all curly in the end, though.

I looked out the window and saw that the snow had stopped. It was then I noticed two women talking outside. When I first looked out, they had hugged, but now they were both smiling with a laugh now and then. One of the women I recognized as Jacqueline Pennington. She sure had recovered from her mother's death quickly. Is that being judgmental? It's true. Or does truth matter when making judgments about people? And does it matter *more* or less if said person is a suspect in a murder? These were questions I still struggled with in my so far vain attempts at losing my judgmental nature.

I studied Jacqueline while she talked outside— something I never had time for before. She wore another expensive pant suit, and I recognized on her arm a Louis Vuitton purse which cost several thousand dollars. Jacqueline Pennington must be good at what she does. Her hair was in a bob or a page boy, whatever they are calling those these days. It was above her shoulders and tucked under, and she wore long bangs. Did she look like a killer? Did any killers look like killers? That was something I was still trying to figure out. I was still looking at her and pondering those questions, when she bade goodbye to her friend, turned, opened the door, and entered the historical society.

CHAPTER FIFTEEN

"HELLO, JACQUELINE," I said as she closed the door behind her.

"Hello. You have me at a disadvantage. I don't know your name."

I stood up, introduced myself, and shook her hand. "I'm sorry about your mother."

She sighed, and I noticed that it looked like she had been crying. "My mother has been sick for years and had been expected to die anytime."

"Yes, I remember that she talked about 'croaking' when she first came in here last year."

Jacqueline smiled, but it was a sad smile. "Yes, she liked saying that for effect."

The woman in front of me looked in her early forties, but her mother looked late eighties. "If you don't mind my saying, you must have been a late baby."

"No, my mother looked much older than she was. Smoking. It makes you look old. She smoked all her life, had emphysema, and toward the end after she got the oxygen tank, she would disconnect it and light up. Mother never thought her life was worth much, and she made every effort to end it early. But she never expected it to end like it did." Jacqueline nodded and added, "She would have been disappointed that she didn't get to solve the puzzle before she died."

"What puzzle?"

"Who killed her uncle. She claimed her father did not do it, and she vowed that some day she would find out who did and bring him or her to justice."

"Him or *her*? Is that what your mother said or is that your take on it?" This confirmed my belief that the sister did it. And that still didn't preclude Jacqueline from killing her own mother.

"Oh, that was her. She always said 'him or her' from the beginning. My earliest memories are of her talking about getting justice done." Jacqueline glanced toward the back and grimaced. "Is it all cleaned up back there?"

Nodding, I said, "Yes, my son took care of that."

"He works here, too?"

I smiled. "Not exactly. He's seven." When she gave me an uneasy glance, I quickly said, "I'm not into child labor or anything! He *volunteered*, because he thought it would be fun to clean up a crime scene. But when he finished, he assured me that was *not* what he wanted to do when he grew up."

Jacqueline smiled. "He sounds cute."

"Yeah, he's a sweetheart. The light of my life. Do you have any children?"

"No. I've been taking care of mother my whole life. I never had time for a husband or a child. My job was the only solace I ever got—the only time I could be away from her."

Let me see. The reasons for her being a suspect were mounting. First, money. Both she and her mother wore very expensive clothing, obviously bought with the mother's money. Second, the old woman tied her down and kept her from fully living her own life. Then I remembered the comment she had made the first time she came in looking for her mother last year, "Nobody signs up for this." Two motives, and they were good ones. "Well, maybe now you'll have time," I said, thinking to myself—unless you're in jail. Not much to choose from in jail.

She shook her head and frowned. "Is it all right if I go back now?"

"Of course. No problem."

She turned and walked toward the exhibits in the back. I wasn't sure if she wanted to see where her mother was killed or the exhibit. But just in case I could squeeze more information out of her, I followed her back.

Standing in front of the exhibit, she sniffed. That made me think even more that she was guilty—trying to make me believe that she was on the verge of tears. I could sniff, too. Here I go. But before I could fake a sniff, I looked at her and watched a single silent tear slide down her face. Oh, well, that still doesn't mean anything.

"My mother spent her entire life, no *wasted* her entire life, searching for a clue to who killed her uncle and framed her father."

"Really?" I asked. "That's why she kept coming in looking at the exhibit?"

Jacqueline nodded. "She thought maybe you had a piece of evidence that would make it definitive."

"Did she say who she thought had done it?"

"Oh, she talked around it. I had my suspicions, but I was never sure, and I think she wanted to keep me guessing. Or else, she was still guessing. It could have been that, too, I guess." She shook her head. "Poor old woman. A totally wasted life."

"Maybe she left a hint somewhere of who she thought it was. Maybe now you'll find it."

"The reading of the will won't be until next week, but I doubt if it will say anything there. It will be a short reading, that much I know."

"What do you mean?"

"She had nothing! I've been supporting her all these years. She wasted not only her life, but all her money on her crazy quest for justice."

I took a step backwards. That blew that motive right there. Jacqueline supported her mother, not the other way around. But in my mind, that still didn't clear her. "Do you think her father really did it?"

She drew in a long breath and slowly let it out. "No. I really don't. I've read enough of my mother's research to believe that much."

I didn't know why, but I had the urge to tell her what I thought—that the two murders were related somehow. Because I *liked* the woman. But again, that didn't preclude her from being a killer. There were several killers who were very charming. "I, um, kind of think the two murders are related. You know, your mother *and* her uncle."

Turning, she looked at me and knotted her brow. "That does make a certain amount of sense, doesn't it? Well, I guess that gets me off the hook, then, I was sick in the bathroom. And I wanted to apologize to you for stinking the place up so bad."

Not mentioning that she wasn't born yet to have anything to do with the first murder, I did say, "Yeah, but can't you buy fake stink at novelty stores?" It was the critical instant. Would she confess right here, now that I had her cornered? Or would she pull a gun and kill me, too? It made me think maybe I should be more careful.

Instead, she looked thoughtful for a minute and said, "Yes! Stink bombs! Fake stink!"

CHAPTER SIXTEEN

MY HEART AND my mind raced at the thought. Nodding, I said, "Stink bombs. That would work." Silence followed, and when I began to think maybe she would pull out a gun and shoot me, I hoped that she would leave Petra out of it.

But she surprised me. "Lorry Lockharte?"

"Yes, that's right."

"Of the Rutledge Lockhartes?" Of course she would know about that. Her family had lived here for decades. When I nodded, she said, "If you're of the Rutledge Lockhartes, then what are you doing working here?"

I couldn't help myself. I laughed. "Because I hate golf! And I wanted something else to do!"

She joined in my laughter. "I hear you there. I can't stand golf either!" Then she looked back at the exhibit. "Well, I see nothing here that would give me a clue as to either my mother's murder or my great uncle's murder. Time to get back to work." Strolling down the hall toward the front, she turned as she got to the door. "I'll let you know if there are any clues in the will."

Right behind her, I said, "Thanks. I'd appreciate that. Bye."

I plopped down in my chair completely confused. She was so pleasant! And she offered to let me know about clues in her mother's will. Plus, as I found out a minute ago, *she* was supporting her mother. Nothing made sense anymore. Sam was right. I needed clarity.

Although I was tempted to look up Sedona vortexes right then, instead I decided to leave that to Aiden when he arrived after school. The scanning wouldn't get done by itself, and I really ought to do it.

"So that was the woman's daughter, huh?" asked Petra, as I walked by her desk.

"Yup. And she's much too pleasant to have committed the murder of her mother and wasn't born yet to kill her great uncle."

"Too pleasant doesn't cut it, Lorry. Remember Ted Bundy? I read a book about him. He was an absolute charmer. So don't let *pleasant* fool you."

I stopped in front of her desk. "Do you have a *feeling* about this, Petra?" Although I knew I was ready to grab onto anything at that moment, I figured I might as well go with it. "Do *you* think she did it?"

"I'm not the one investigating this, Lorry. I leave that to you. I'm just sayin' not to let pleasant dissuade you from the absolute truth."

Disappointed, I nodded and walked toward the stairs. When I got to my upstairs desk, partially to help my clarity and partially because I couldn't leave it alone, instead of working on the *Children* binder, I picked up the binder with the murder in it and started reading and scanning.

Between pages, I thought of what Petra had said about not letting pleasant dissuade me from the absolute truth, and I realized she was right. I could be wrong about the same person doing both murders. It was obvious that I needed to keep an open mind. But I felt confident that tomorrow at the vortex would help me. At least Sam thought it would, and I had to hope she was right.

Hours passed, and I wouldn't have even noticed except that I heard Petra call me from the bottom of the stairs. "Hey, Lorry! Billy just called and said he left you a message on your cell."

"Thanks, Petra!"

After I finished scanning the document I was working on, I marked my place and proceeded downstairs to my desk. Billy usually called on my cell instead of the historical society business phone because he knew I was upstairs instead of at my regular desk where the phone was. No matter how many times I told him that I kept my cell in my purse in the bottom drawer of the downstairs desk, he somehow imagined that I kept it with me. So I plunked myself down at my desk, opened the drawer, pulled my cell phone from my purse, and punched his number.

"Hi, sweetheart. Listen, I was going to ask you to have Aiden call me when he got in, but then I realized it would save time and effort to just email you what I needed. So I did that! Love you! See you later! Bye!"

I shook my head and to myself, I said, "Bye, Billy. I love you, too." Then I chuckled, put the phone away, and checked my email. He had sent me an email listing where he wanted to go tomorrow and asking Aiden to plan the trip for us. Zack, who was going to college to be a computer expert, had spent some time teaching Aiden a thing or two about the computer. Plus, Aiden had computer studies at school, although I think they taught him different stuff from what Zack taught him. I wasn't sure if I even wanted to know what Zack taught him, but so far, no matter what I asked Aiden to do—computer-wise—he did it. After printing out what Billy wanted, I added what *I* wanted and in the order that I wanted it, and left the note on the desk for Aiden for when he arrived.

Returning upstairs, I worked on the scanning—and the re-reading of the murder documents—until Aiden came in a little while later. He bounded upstairs and jumped into my arms, with Bingo yipping at his heels.

"Hi, Mommy!"

"Hi, sweetie. How was school today?"

"Good, as usual. How was work today?"

"It was fine." We went through this routine every day, which felt silly, because if something big happened at work—like the murder—Aiden had already heard about it before he ever arrived. "Listen, kiddo, Sheriff Billy has something he wants you to look up on the computer. And I also added a few things to it. It's on my desk downstairs."

"Okay, Mommy." He looked at me seriously. "You know, Mommy, that after you and Sheriff Billy get married, I will be calling him Sheriff Daddy."

"Yes, I know."

"So, I was thinking that you should start getting used to it."

Quickly swallowing the chuckle that tried to form in my throat, I said, "Oh. You think so?" When he nodded, I said, "Well, maybe you're right. Since tomorrow we're on a trip to investigate a location for the ceremony, perhaps Sheriff Billy will allow you—just for tomorrow, until we get married, you understand—to call him Sheriff Daddy."

Aiden brightened, and his whole face turned into one big smile. He slid off my lap so he could see my face better. "Really? You think he'd let me?"

Smiling back at him, I reached out and pulled him back into my arms. "I just think he might, Aiden, I think he might."

CHAPTER SEVENTEEN

SATURDAY MORNING BILLY picked us up early and drove us over to Martha and Hugo's house for breakfast. Billy had suggested we all go out to breakfast, but Martha insisted on eating at her house. She said she wasn't sure if they would be able to eat lunch out anywhere because of Hugo's keto diet, so she wanted them to have a good breakfast.

When we sat down at the table, Martha served us each a three-egg omelet with olives, cheese, and mushrooms in it, with bacon on the side. I never thought Aiden could finish such a big portion, but he dug right in.

"Oh, my goodness, Martha! *This* is a diet? It's delicious!"

"If it doesn't taste good, then I won't eat! So we make every meal taste like a treat!" Hugo said in his silly rhymes.

"It definitely tastes good, Hugo," said Billy.

Aiden took a breath between mouthfuls. "Grammy? Grampy? I've got something to tell you. Sheriff Billy said that since we were looking for a location for the wedding today, it was all right if I called him Sheriff Daddy. I just wanted to let you know."

Billy had told him that in the car. We both knew how happy that made him, but didn't realize he was just bursting to tell someone.

Aiden went back to eating, and no one said anything for a beat or two. Billy and I looked at each other. Then Hugo said, "Well, Aiden, I understand that. How 'bout if you call me Sheriff Grampy?"

Aiden laughed. "I would, Grampy, but you're not the sheriff!"

We finished eating; I helped Martha clean up; and then we walked out the front door. Martha looked at Billy's big truck parked in the driveway and frowned. "Say, Billy. I know your truck is comfortable and all, but how about if we take our car? You can drive."

Hugo and Martha owned a late-model Cadillac. When they opened the garage and Hugo backed it out beside Billy's truck, it looked surprisingly like any other car. I remember many years ago when Cadillacs looked different from most other cars. This one looked like *a car*.

Hugo stepped out and held the door open for Billy. Before getting in, Billy said, "You sure about this? I think my truck is bigger for all of us."

Martha smiled. "This will be more comfortable for all of us, Billy. Go ahead. It's okay. You drive."

She thought Billy was uncomfortable about driving their vehicle, but I knew Billy better than that. He *loved* his truck, and he loved any opportunity to drive it. This situation would upset him, but he would never show it. Nobody would ever suspect how disappointed he was.

Hugo got in back with Martha, who had already climbed in, but I stopped him. "No, Hugo, you sit in the front with Billy. Martha and I and Aiden can sit in the back."

I was about to get in when I noticed Aiden standing to the side looking dejected. "Aiden, what is it, sweetie?"

He held out the piece of paper that he had written all the instructions on. "I thought I was going to sit in the front and navigate."

"Aiden, you know you can't sit in the front until you're bigger," I said, trying to sound understanding. I wanted to get going.

But Billy heard what was going on. "Aiden, son, you *are* the navigator. But you need to sit in the back with your mommy and Grammy. Okay? You still get to be the navigator. I wouldn't dream of replacing you with Grampy. He'd sing all the directions in rhyme, and I wouldn't know where to go!"

Aiden nodded and laughed and crawled in beside Martha. Billy always knew just what to say to him. What a great father he will be. I climbed in, checked Aiden's seat belt, and fastened my own, while Billy backed out of the driveway. He looked in the rearview mirror. "Which way now, navigator?"

"To Coyote Moon! You know the way!"

"Y'all know that I wanted to go over the mountain to Sedona today. But we can't do that driving this fancy contraption."

Martha looked at me, rolled her eyes, and mouthed the words, "Thank, goodness!"

"But, Billy," I said, "it snowed yesterday. It would be all slippery."

"Let's take the mountain!" said Aiden, looking at all his notes that had directions from Rutledge to Cottonwood.

"Yeah, this vehicle will make it! Let's do it!" said Hugo. "Over the mountain, straight and true. This Cadillac will get there for you!"

"Slip on the road, which will give me a frown. We'd end up in the canyon, upside down!" I said. Then added, "Hey, I can rhyme, too. That wasn't half bad!"

Martha reached over and patted my arm, Aiden giggled, and Billy said, "All right, all right. Coyote Moon it is. Let's go."

Hugo and Billy talked in the front, Martha and I talked in the back, and Aiden read over and over the notes he had made. When we arrived at the highway where we should turn, Aiden raised his voice and said, "*Navigator says,* turn left here to go south toward Cottonwood!"

"Yes, *sir*," said Billy. "Right away, *sir*," as he made the turn.

And our journey had begun.

CHAPTER EIGHTEEN

THE HIGHWAY FROM Coyote Moon to Cottonwood was a two-lane blacktop. It cut through high desert which I knew I would see a lot of today. We wouldn't be seeing much civilization until we got to Cottonwood, and when we arrived in Cottonwood, there would be too much civilization.

When the conversation waned after we had been driving a while, I examined the Cadillac. Billy looked comfortable enough behind the wheel, but had he been sitting back here, there wouldn't be enough room for his long legs and big feet. They would be crimped under the seat. And although the seats were comfortable, they weren't any more comfortable than the seats in Billy's truck, maybe even less so. Billy's truck, a Ford King Ranch, with a sunroof and leather interior was the most expensive model and felt like it. This Cadillac probably was, too—it had leather interior as well—but it didn't have the charm and appeal of Billy's truck. Although, I smiled to myself, maybe part of the appeal of Billy's truck was that Billy was always driving it.

We arrived in Cottonwood, and Billy said, "Okay, navigator. Which way now?" He expected Aiden to say "89A toward Sedona," but that's not what happened.

The additions I had made to the list changed Billy's plans, and I had neglected to mention them to Billy last night. Did I do that on purpose? No, not really. I didn't think Billy would object. But after the three of us played a hot game of Ticket to Ride, Billy had gone home.

"No, Sheriff Daddy, take 260 toward Camp Verde."

Billy glanced in the rearview mirror first at Aiden, then at me, then back at Aiden. "Are you *sure*, little pard?"

"Yup," I said. "He's sure."

"Aha!" said Billy. "Now I understand." He smiled back at both of us and cruised onto 260.

"Mommy added stuff to your list, Sheriff Daddy. That's all."

We passed the Verde Valley Fire Department on the left and a few miles farther down the road, we passed a big car dealership on the right. There were multiple traffic circles on this route, or roundabouts, as the British would say. It was also high desert—there was a lot of that around here—but there were places they may be planning more housing developments. Too many people and not enough land. We passed an indoor shooting range and a sign for Out of Africa. I had heard that was a cool place, but I had never been there. It was not a zoo, which was a good thing. And they had a zipline there, that ran above the animals. I made a mental note that we should go sometime.

When we approached the interstate, Aiden raised his voice, "*Navigator says*, get in the left lane to head north on I-17 toward Flag."

"Got it, little pard."

Billy slid into the left lane, turned left, and headed down the on-ramp. Then he merged smoothly into traffic, and we were closer to our destination. Which, honestly, I wasn't that excited about, and neither was Billy. Getting married in some fancy church? That's just not who Billy and I were, but we were both trying to appease Martha and Hugo. And I wasn't even sure why we were doing that. They wouldn't have minded if we said we just wanted something simple. For Martha, though, she wanted to make it a special day for us. But I was marrying Billy Madrigal! That was special enough!

In a few more minutes, Aiden announced, "*Navigator says*, get off at exit 298 for Highway 179 toward Sedona."

Martha leaned toward me, over Aiden's head, and pretended to whisper, "Can that kid get any cuter?" Aiden squirmed in his seat and smiled but didn't say anything.

Billy exited the interstate and followed the sign at the bottom that had an arrow pointing to the left and said *Sedona* on top and *Oak Creek Canyon* on the bottom. Aiden said, "Left here, Daddy," and then caught himself and quickly corrected, "I mean, Sheriff Daddy."

"Watch it, youngster!" said Billy in a mock mean voice.

But Aiden was subdued, and I hoped he didn't take Billy's comment seriously, because *I knew* he was just kidding. Maybe Aiden didn't know, so I leaned over and whispered in his ear, "Aiden, Billy was just kidding."

He stuck out his chin, nodded, and said, "I know," but still looked sad. Aiden was a great kid, mature for his age, happy, healthy mentally and physically, but he did have a *history*. And sometimes, something odd could set him off, and I wondered if this was one of those times. So I put my arm around him, pulled him close, and kissed him on the top of his head. I'd have to say something *privately* to Billy when we got out of the car. Then I noticed that Billy was looking at us in the rearview mirror, and I realized that I wouldn't have to say anything to him. He was sensitive enough to see Aiden's reaction, and he'd take care of it. That was my Billy. I wouldn't do anything to jeopardize our relationship.

Looking out the window, I saw a sign *Sedona 15* and shortly after that a sign announcing the *Coconino National Forest*. Then a few minutes later, we passed the ranger station on the right. And it wasn't long after that we could see the first hint of the full majesty of the red rocks.

"Ah, now I see why you wanted to come this way, Lorry. It's beautiful, and this way we can see it from both directions," said Billy.

"The rocks here are red, the rocks here are blue. But either way, you know I love you!" said Hugo, turning around to look at Martha, who smiled back at him.

"No, Grampy. No blue rocks here." And to Billy, he said, "No, Sheriff Daddy. Mommy wanted to go to the Bell Rock vortex—whatever that is. I didn't have time to google it."

And all eyes turned toward me. What did I get myself into?

CHAPTER NINETEEN

WE HAD GONE through several traffic circles and my answer to their curious looks was delayed indefinitely when Aiden announced. "Here, Sheriff Billy! Turn here into the Bell Rock parking lot."

Billy slowed the car and pulled in. "You're sure *this* is where you want to go, Lorry?"

"Yes, Billy, I'm sure."

"All right, then." He drove slowly, looking around. Then he saw a sign that said, *Fee Station Buy Passes Here*, so he stopped the car and reached into his pocket for his wallet. "Aiden, can you climb over your mom and pay our ransom?"

Aiden unfastened his seat belt and reached for the five dollar bill that Billy held up. "Sure, Sheriff Daddy. Sorry I called you Sheriff Billy before."

"No worries, kiddo. I'm just going to park up here. Okay?"

I opened the door of the car, and Aiden crawled gently over me. He ran to the Fee Station, and I looked at what I would have to call a very informal concession stand. All they sold were sun hats, and they were the floppy canvas variety. The only semi-cowboyish hat they had was a green camo with one side of the brim snapped onto the crown. Billy wouldn't wear that hat if you gave him a million dollars. He already had a million dollars, but even so. He wouldn't.

And the person tending the dime-store table filled with hats looked more middle eastern than Native American. This was the kind of place you'd expect to see *cowboys and Indians*. But no cowboy hats and no Native Americans. Well, maybe he was from India, which would at least make him Indian. That would work.

Billy parked the car a few spots down, and Aiden came running back with the five dollar bill still in his hand. "Sheriff Daddy! It's cards only!"

Billy took the bill out of Aiden's hand and pulled a card out of his wallet as he walked toward the machine. I waited for Martha and Hugo to get out of the car. Looking around, I realized why the guy at the hat stand didn't look Native American. There was a hand-lettered sign attached to the front of the table that read *International Society for KRSNA Consciousness*. And yes, I spelled that right. And it explained everything, including the lack of cowboy and Indian garb.

"What are we doing here?" asked Martha. "I don't see anything except that." She motioned toward the start of the trail.

"Um, wow, yeah," was all I could think to say. Bell Rock, this huge monolith that looked like a bell, was not anywhere close to where we were. I had assumed— wrongly as I now saw—that it would be close to the parking area, and I could just skip on over to it, get my clarity, and leave. That was not the way it was going to be. Pointing over my shoulder, I said, "I need to get to that."

Billy returned from the machine, and after putting the receipt on the dashboard of the car and locking it, he walked over to us. Aiden was looking at the big map on display. Billy looked around and then looked at me. "Lorry? What are you up to now? This is a hiking trail! Look at your shoes!"

I looked down, already aware of what I would see even before my head made the effort. Three-inch heels. Of course. My standard footwear. "I didn't expect it to be so far. But I have to at least try." You can't imagine how much I wanted that clarity.

But now I also looked down at my clothes. I had on a yellow pantsuit that matched the yellow heels. It wasn't ideal for hiking, but it was too late to think of that. Martha wasn't in hiking attire, either. She wore a light blue pantsuit, very stylish, with light blue flats. Hugo, who, when he was grossly overweight, always wore loose-fitting sweatpants, now wore beige dockers with a light blue shirt that matched Martha's outfit. They did that sometimes. I thought it was cute, but I didn't think Billy would do it. Billy wore tight black jeans and a green and black cowboy shirt that made him look even better than usual. Of course, Billy's six foot four frame looked good in almost anything. He'd even look good in a tutu! That image almost made me laugh, but I stifled it. Aiden was always ready for hiking. Today he wore blue jeans and a sweatshirt with an aardvark on it, which said *A is for Aardvark*.

"Martha? Hugo? I don't suppose you want to hike out there with us." He handed Hugo the key to the car. "You can sit over there or get in the car." Then he leaned over and whispered in Hugo's ear loud enough for me to hear. "I don't think we'll be long."

Not wanting to wait for Hugo's answer, I strode confidently toward the trail. Aiden saw me and followed along. A second after that, Billy showed up and put his hand on my elbow.

"What are you doing?" I asked.

"Making sure you don't go butt over teakettle."

I would have pulled my arm away and huffed off after saying something bordering on rude, but at that moment, my heel got caught in the uneven trail, and I was pitched forward. The only thing that saved me was Billy's grip on my elbow. So instead of saying something smart-alecky, I said, "Thank you," and kept walking.

But after we had walked a few more minutes, and I realized what a rocky uneven trail it was *and* how far away Bell Rock was, not to mention after Billy had saved me from landing on my knees two more times, I decided we should go back. "Aiden!"

"I want to keep hiking!"

"Aiden, I can't go with you because I need to help your mother, and you can't go on alone. Come on! Let's go!"

Aiden kicked a small stone out of his way, frowned, and turned around. "*O-kay.*" He drew it out letting us know that he was not happy.

The way back was worse than the way out, probably because I was in a hurry to return. On one of my many stumbles, I almost went to my knees before Billy hauled me up. But I returned in one piece to find Martha and Hugo unlocking the car.

"Lorry, I'm going to the restroom. You want to go?"

91

"No, thanks. I'll wait for the chapel. Aiden? Do you have to go?"

When Aiden said no, Billy got a smirk on his face and said, "What? You're not going to ask me? What am I? Chopped liver?"

"Chopped liver I am and I will be, even though I don't really have to pee," sang Hugo, who followed Martha to the restrooms.

When they returned, Martha said, "It was fine, Lorry, if you have to go. Very clean." But Hugo frowned and pinched off his nose between his finger and thumb.

"No, I'm good. Let's get going." I was eager to get to the chapel. Honestly, I didn't think it was going to work out, but once it didn't, then we could move on and figure out the *right thing*.

CHAPTER TWENTY

IT WAS ONLY a few minutes later back on Highway 179, that Bell Rock appeared, and it was so close to the road that I felt like I could reach out and touch it. Unfortunately there were signs that said *No Stopping or Parking*. So I did what I could—I pressed the button to unroll the window and stuck both arms outside reaching toward Bell Rock trying to absorb the energy, as Sam would call it. Although I didn't understand it, I was ready to try anything to get clarity.

We were past it in no time, and Aiden, still beside me, said, "Sheriff Daddy! Turn here into the other Bell Rock parking lot. Maybe it will get Mommy closer so she doesn't have to hike so far."

Billy pulled in and parked right at the trailhead. All of us exited the car again, and I started up the trail. It was much smoother than the previous trail but not rockless. So when Billy came up and gently grabbed my elbow, I was grateful. We came around a corner of the trail, and I saw how far we were from Bell Rock. I stopped abruptly, taking Billy off guard. He almost went down and me with him. But he didn't, and I didn't, and I told him I wanted to turn around. We had to wait for Aiden, though, who had run ahead on the trail. When he realized we weren't following, he came right back.

As we got into the car, I realized that my arms hanging out of the car a few minutes ago would be the closest I'd come to Bell Rock—today, and probably forever. We all piled into the car—Martha and Hugo had waited at the trailhead for us—and took off. Not too much later, we passed a sign for Little Horse Trailhead.

"Horses!" said Aiden. "Pull in there Sheriff Daddy! Please?"

"You know, Aiden, it's just a trailhead. There are no horses there," I told him.

But when we pulled around the circular parking lot, there at the far end was a horse trailer. "Yes, there are! See!" He strained at his seat belt trying to see the horses, but they were off somewhere trotting down the trail.

Billy looked in the rearview mirror with a funny glint in his eyes. "You like horses, Aiden?"

"Yeah! Do you see them?" He strained at his seat belt again, but had no luck in finding them, so he settled down beside me.

"No, I think they're off wandering the trails right now, little pard." Billy deftly turned the car back onto the highway to Sedona.

Not long after that, we passed a sign for a trailhead called Indian Cliffs. Hugo said, "Aiden, I suppose you want to stop here to see the Indians." He said it jokingly and meant no harm by it. Then he added, "But I guess that's politically incorrect, isn't it?"

Aiden looked at him and said, "I know a lot of people make fun of politically correct, but actually it's just being kind and not making fun of people who are different from us."

"That's very wise, Aiden," said Martha. "Did you learn that in school?"

Aiden shook his head. "No. From reading." No one said anything more until Aiden said, "Sheriff Daddy, up here on the right. Chapel Road."

Billy turned and drove farther than I thought we should. "Are you sure this is it, Aiden?"

"Yup. Chapel Road. Sure."

"Yeah, Aiden's right. It's up here."

Then it came into view. The street narrowed, and we passed a sign on the right. *Chapel of the Holy Cross* and then beneath that in smaller letters *Catholic Chapel* and *Diocese of Phoenix*. Then the sign had the hours—standard business hours, nine to five—and beneath that it had four little pictures with lines through them. The top row had a car towing a trailer and a bus. The bottom row had a cigarette and something I couldn't readily identify. "What is that on the bottom? A machine gun?"

Everyone laughed, but no one but Aiden knew what it was. Billy might have, but his eyes were on the narrow road. "No, Mommy, not a machine gun! It's a drone! No drones allowed!"

We proceeded slowly, because of so many people milling around. And then I saw it. A big triangular yellow sign that said *STOP. These are the only PUBLIC RESTROOMS. None In Chapel.* Uh oh. The *restrooms*, as they called them, were the kind you see at construction sites, except these looked old and rickety and liable to fall over if you blew a fart. Has that been too much bathroom talk for this story? Sorry. I won't do it again.

But I did realize that I was in trouble. Crossing my legs, I grimaced and hoped we could get out in a hurry.

Billy pulled into a parking space across from the restrooms. "Anybody gotta go?" He turned around and looked at me.

I cleared my throat. "I can wait. Those don't look safe."

"Oh, Lorry!" said Billy.

"I gotta go!" said Aiden.

"Be careful!" I said, as Aiden crawled over my lap.

Billy got out to walk him across the busy street. They each got into a line in front of one of the restrooms—if you could call them that—and I crossed my fingers that the things wouldn't blow over before they got out. But a few minutes later, they were safely back in the car.

"Should we leave the car here or try to get a parking place farther up?"

"We better try to get one higher," said Martha. "This is a long, steep walk."

"All righty, then," Billy said as he carefully backed up.

We made our way up the narrow street with cars parked on both sides. I hoped there was a place for us to turn around if we didn't find a parking place up there. Although it would have been a tough climb up the steep road in my heels, I thought I saw a small courtesy cart drive by carrying several tourists.

"There's a spot there! Sheriff Daddy! Up there on the left!"

"How does he see those when I can't even see them?" asked Martha.

Aiden smiled. "When you're good, you're good." That comment sent all of us into peals of laughter.

Billy pulled smoothly in, and we all exited the vehicle. Aiden wanted to run up the hill, but I made him hold my hand. There were cars going up and down in tight spaces, cars turning around, and probably none of them paying good attention to the pedestrians all along the path. Billy came up beside me and took my other hand. Martha and Hugo walked behind us, also hand in hand. Billy and I were about to find out if this would be the place we would get married. Wasn't life grand?

CHAPTER TWENTY-ONE

IT WAS A beautiful chapel, nestled into the rocks like that. Too bad the walk up to it was such a chore. Martha, Hugo, and I were all huffing and puffing, but Aiden and Billy didn't even notice the steep incline. At least Martha was smart enough to have worn flats today. My heels weren't helping my ability to navigate the steep climb. Lucky for me, Billy and Aiden held on tight so I couldn't fall.

Near the entrance, there was a big sign that had their hours posted, a cigarette with a red line through it that said, *Smoke Free Environment*, and what I didn't need a reminder of *No public restrooms in chapel*.

When we got to the entrance—a narrow path maybe steeper than the driveway we had just walked—I stopped and held onto the rail. "Maybe we should wait a minute so Martha and Hugo can catch their breath." But I think I was breathing harder than the two of them put together. Hugo just winked at me, although he leaned on the rail, too.

Aiden looked up at me and tugged at my hand. "Mommy, can I go up while you're resting?"

"No, you need to wait until we're at least on our way."

"Pl-ease?" he said in two syllables. "There are no cars here, and if someone tries to grab me, I'll scream!" Billy and I had taught the boy well.

Stepping forward, Billy grabbed Aiden and swung him over the railing. "What if someone picks you up and throws you to the rocks below, and you don't have a chance to scream?" There were no rocks below where we were. Billy held him over the cement walk on the other side of us.

"I'll karate chop him and hold on for dear life!"

Billy swung him back over the railing, set him on his feet, and said, "Good man. But your Mommy has to give you the okay."

Aiden jumped up and down and said, "Please, Mommy, please? I'll be fine! It's church!"

"That doesn't necessarily mean that bad things can't happen here, Aiden." I looked at Martha and Hugo who seemed to be breathing normally again. "But go ahead. I think we've all rested enough." Aiden raced ahead, and we walked to the other side of the rail and started climbing the steep path.

There were signs along the way warning people not to climb on the rocks. As we ascended the twisty path, I had one hand on the railing and Billy had the other. At the top, finally, I took a minute to catch my breath and look around at how beautiful everything was. Red rocks surrounded the chapel, and the urban sprawl was depressing and ugly. It was a great juxtaposition: the beauty of the red rocks and the ugliness of the sprawl. Trying to think of happier things, I saw Bell Rock to the east. Aiden stood in front of the railing gazing in that direction. It really was a remarkable rock formation—so much like a bell.

Martha and Hugo, who had been trailing behind, caught up to us. "Are you two ready to go in?"

"Yeah," said Hugo. "We want to see if we can get you right hitched up."

"Aiden, come on," I said. I took his hand, and we walked past a fountain on the way into the chapel. As we approached the heavy metal door that reached the ceiling of the chapel, there was a sign that said *Peace to All Who Enter. Please maintain silence in the chapel.* I pointed it out to Aiden, and he looked at me, nodded, and then swiped his thumb and forefinger across his mouth in a zipping motion. I smiled at him and thought how lucky I was to have a cute kid like that.

Billy came up behind me and said, "Considering we might get married here, I think we should walk in together." He took my hand, I smiled and nodded, and we walked in together, with Martha and Hugo trailing behind, and Aiden out in front.

The chapel was in a beautiful spot, perched up here in the rocks. But I could see that for this place, at least, it was location location location. The inside of the chapel was unadorned and almost utilitarian. One would expect beautiful stained glass windows inside, but one would be disappointed. There were none. Straight ahead there was a huge stylized tree with J.C. spread out on it. There were some wall hangings that were unimpressive, and if one didn't know what a beautiful spot it was built in, it would be an unremarkable church.

Plain wooden benches with padded kneelers were on each side of a narrow aisle down the center of the church. To the right as we walked in was an area filled with rows of red candle holders with white candles, some lit, some not. A sign, posted over a machine that accepted money, said *Votive Candles $1 Credit Cards Accepted*. To our left was a low wall with some holy water in a flat, square container. But the chapel was filled with people and too many people walking by had caused a stray hair to land in the water. Did that make it a holy hair? I didn't know, but I wasn't going to touch it to find out.

As Billy and I looked around, and Aiden wandered around looking at everything, I felt a tap on my shoulder. Martha motioned to our left. I saw a sign that said *Gift Shop Downstairs*. I nodded to Billy and the sign, and he nodded that he understood. But Aiden was at the front of the church looking behind velvet barriers where a table with a white, gold-trimmed tablecloth sat on a pedestal. There was no way to get his attention without going to get him.

Hugo tapped me on the shoulder then, and pointed to himself and to Aiden, which I took to mean that he would go get him. Nodding, I led Billy and Martha down the stairs. Three quarters of the way down the stairs, I saw an AED device on the wall. AED equals Automatic External Defibrillator. And I thought—no wonder! Having to walk up that steep driveway and steep walkway could give anyone a heart attack! Might as well be prepared!

Before I continued into the crowded gift shop, I looked up to see Billy and Martha smiling at me. Aiden was higher up looking over the barrier. He and Hugo had not passed the landing yet. On the gift shop door, it said, *No Public Restrooms Turn off cell phones while in gift shop*. Martha and I didn't carry ours, but I saw Billy reach into his pocket, pull his out, tap a couple of times, and slide it back into his pocket. I made my way into the gift shop.

Aiden ran through the door and threw his arms around me. "I missed you, Mommy!" Then he threw his arms around Billy. "I missed you, Sheriff Daddy!" Billy picked him up and, unable to swing him around in the tight quarters, put him back down. Aiden looked around. "I'm going over there."

"Just stay in the gift shop, Aiden," I said.

Martha stepped up to me. "I wanted to come in here because there was no one up there to talk to about the wedding." She looked around. "And it looks like the only people in here are the cashiers."

Looking around, I saw what she meant. There were two cashiers to the right of us, with a long line leading to a central exit point. "I guess we ask them." The line looked daunting, but there was no other choice. They both looked overwhelmed, and I didn't want to stress them by asking them a question while they worked. "I'll go."

I turned around, kissed Billy, and walked around the display cases in the middle of the store toward the end of the line. The store was a mix of religious items and Arizona tourist items, but mostly religious. Aiden had settled in front of a display of touristy items with the state of Arizona printed on it. He had put one thimble on each of his ten fingers and held them up to himself admiringly. It made me smile. What a great kid he was. Martha and Hugo were looking at the various items, but I looked around and didn't see Billy anywhere. Suddenly I felt lips on my neck, and there he was with a big smile on his face.

"You know," he whispered, "this isn't my ideal wedding place."

Nodding and smiling, I whispered back, "I totally agree, but we have to appease Martha and Hugo." The line had moved up several spots, and we went with it. "And we can hope they say no." He nodded enthusiastically, and then we stood in line in silence until we arrived at the front a few minutes later.

"Can I help you?" asked the smiling but stressed woman with short gray hair.

"Yes, can you tell me if it's possible to get married here?" I glanced up at my handsome fiancé to show her how lucky I was.

"Yes, it is. You have to go through the church of St. John Vianney."

I nodded. That didn't sound too difficult. I figured it was in Sedona. But it didn't change anything, because it wasn't where Billy and I wanted to get married.

Then she added, "And you have to go through classes."

"Oh," I said.

Then Billy spoke up and cleared up the whole matter quickly. "Do you have to be Catholic?"

The woman nodded eagerly, like she expected us to want to convert just so we could get married there. "Yes, you do!"

Luckily Billy spoke up. "All right, thank you very much for your help." Then he guided me out the door. I say luckily because I might have said something rude to the woman.

"That's not fair!" I looked up at Billy with a scowl on my face. "Just 'cause we're not Catholic. It's not fair! That's religious persecution or something. Isn't it?"

H whispered in my ear, "I didn't think you wanted to get married here."

"Oh, yeah. I don't. You're right." It calmed me down. "Thanks." Billy always knew how to make me feel better.

CHAPTER TWENTY-TWO

AFTER GLANCING AT Aiden to make sure he saw us leaving and motioning with my head for him to bring Martha and Hugo with him, we climbed the stairs. Sometimes I thought Aiden and I could read each other's minds. Because when I motioned with my head, it could have meant *anything*, and yet Aiden nodded his head like he knew *exactly* what I was asking.

We arrived at the top and stepped out of the chapel. Turning around, we saw that Martha, Hugo, and Aiden had followed, as expected.

"Mommy!" he said, once outside. "I love you!" We hugged and then Aiden hugged Billy, too.

We made our way across the courtyard to the top of the path. "Okay, time to eat?" asked Billy.

"No, we have one more stop to make, don't we, Mom?" Aiden said. We walked side by side holding hands. He glanced up at me with a conspiratorial smile.

"Yup."

"You're not going to tell us?" asked Hugo. "Where are we going? Where will it be? You can reveal it to just me!" He pointed to his ear and looked at Aiden.

Aiden smiled and shook his head. "You'll find out soon enough. It won't take long, though, will it Mom? I'm getting hungry."

"No, sweetie, it shouldn't take long." I had no idea how long visiting a vortex and getting clarity would take, but I wouldn't allow it to take too long, because I was hungry, too. And if it turned out to be like Bell Rock, it wouldn't take long at all.

We headed down the steep path. I thought Aiden would want to run down—which I wasn't happy about—but he clung to my hand on one side and Billy's on the other. Maybe he was more bothered by being left behind than he let on. That would be like Aiden not to want me to feel bad. I leaned over and kissed him on the top of his head, and he smiled up at me. Then Billy lifted his arm up and I lifted my arm up, raising Aiden up in the air. He giggled and moved his legs like he was on a unicycle, and we all laughed. Martha and Hugo were close behind and they laughed, too.

Down at the bottom of the path, we still had to negotiate the steep driveway, but it wasn't far. My feet inside my three-inch heels were not feeling good, and I still had to climb up to the vortex, but I was still hoping it wouldn't be far. That one was supposed to be closer to the parking area.

Just before we reached the car, a man stood at the back of his SUV with the door open. He was pouring water into his wide-mouthed water bottle from a gallon container. The top of his bottle fell on the pavement, wrong side down. He looked at us, shrugged his shoulders, and said, "Ah, well, it's holy ground, right?" Then he screwed it into the top of his water bottle without even wiping it off.

106

Aiden said, "Yuck, no. It's *dirty* ground!"

I shrugged back to the man. "From the mouths of babes—" and I continued walking to the car, glad that I had raised my son right. In our house, there was no so-called *three-second rule*. If food landed on the floor, it was for Bingo. Period.

After we had all piled into the car, and Aiden and I were still chuckling over the interaction, Billy smiled at us both and started the car. He eased out of the spot, avoiding the people walking by and the cars parked on the other side of the narrow road.

"See?" said Hugo. "I told ya he could drive!" And that made us all laugh.

There was a reason that Aiden called Martha and Hugo Grammy and Grampy. Besides Billy, they were as close as I had to family. And we always had a good time with them.

We continued on to Sedona, and when we got to the traffic circle in town, Aiden said, "Follow it around and take the exit toward the left."

"We're taking a slight detour, kiddo," Billy said as he headed to the right.

"Oh," said Aiden, surprised. "Okay."

After making the turn, Billy waved his arm in a flamboyant fashion. "And this, ladies and gentlemen, is the famous uptown Sedona."

I'd been here before—who living in Rutledge hasn't? —but I looked around. Signs abounded, and it was clearly a haven for tourists. Restaurants, t-shirt shops, candle stores, information, and the crystals and psychic readings for which Sedona is famous. A few blocks up, the touristy stuff had disappeared, and the road led up into the mountains toward Flagstaff, so Billy turned around.

"That was a short tour," said Hugo.

"That's all there is!" said Billy.

Back at the traffic circle, Billy took the exit that Aiden had mentioned earlier, and we headed southwest on 89A. A few minutes later, Aiden piped up, "Turn left here, Sheriff Daddy! This is it!"

Billy had to pass the Airport Mesa Trailhead on the left, go up the hill, and turn around before we found a parking spot almost right in front of the trailhead.

I released my seat belt and had my hand on the door, when I heard Martha say to Aiden, "Sweetie, why don't you stay here with Grampy and me? I think your mom needs to be alone right now."

Aiden noticed that Billy had already gotten out of the car, so he said, "Sheriff Billy's going."

Hugo, from the front seat, said, "She needs his help to get up the path!"

As much as I hated to admit my weaknesses—and I had a few to admit!—I had to agree with that. "He's right. I do."

"O-kay," Aiden said, clearly disappointed. But he snapped his seat belt back on and put his head on Martha's arm.

When I walked to the front of the car, Billy immediately put his hand under my elbow. "This doesn't look as rough as the Bell Rock trail, but it's no, you know, walk in the park, either." He smiled at me and leaned down and kissed me. "Let's go."

We started up the trail and it split. To the left, a sign said *Summit Trail*. It was steep stairs made out of rock. If we went straight instead, the sign said *Airport Loop–Sedona*

108

View. The trail wasn't as steep and looked easier to walk. No one can accuse me of being a wimp. We took the trail to the left. Aiden's instructions hadn't included exactly where the vortex was, so I was *following my heart*, as my grandmother used to say. Billy looked at both trails and at me, shrugged, and then we started up the hill.

The trail at Bell Rock was populated, but not like this one—probably because we were so close to town. There were people going up, people going down, even people going from side to side. But none of them—not a single one—wore three-inch heels. And I can tell you that I got more than a few odd looks when people saw what I was wearing. But no matter. I'm not going to defend myself. I do what I do.

After we reached the top of a rise, there were informational signs and a trail leading even higher. But I felt compelled to follow the trail to the right.

"Do you know where you're going, Lorry?"

"No, I have no idea, but I think we're almost there."

We walked a little farther up the trail. Billy, who had been to my left holding my elbow and helping me to stay upright, suddenly stepped in front of me and gathered me into his arms. It was a glorious day what with the intensity of the blue sky and the beautiful red rocks all around us. He looked into my eyes and said, "Marry me! Right here! Right now!"

I smiled up at him and kissed him on the lips. "I love you, Billy. And I want to be your wife. It's practically a done deal already. Come on, let's finish up here. I'm getting hungry." Then I pulled away from him and trudged up the rest of the path to a sign that spoke of the vortex. It didn't say that's where the vortex was, but I took it to mean that it was. It did say it wasn't in a

"particular site, but a general area of enhanced energy."
And that was a good thing because when I looked down
at the valley below, I saw evidence of more urban sprawl.
Yuck.

But I stepped away from the sign, closed my eyes, took
a deep breath, tried to relax, and waited for the clarity to
come.

CHAPTER TWENTY-THREE

I KNEW BETTER than to feel impatient. Impatience didn't seem conducive to getting clarity. And after a few minutes of standing there, clarity came. Jacqueline Pennington did not kill her mother. If there was any motive at all, it would be a large insurance settlement. But since Jacqueline was *supporting* her mother, I didn't think there would even be any insurance on the old woman. No, the person who killed Virginia Pennington was the same person who killed Edward Pennington so many decades ago. It had to be. And the banging sound which made the nick in the hard Lexan plastic was because the killer wanted to get the gun out of the exhibit. What else was in there that would be valuable to a killer? It had to be the gun. Color me clarified.

After taking another deep breath, I opened my eyes and smiled at Billy. "Let's go. I'm hungry."

He kissed me on the lips, put his arm around me for a quick hug, and we walked down the trail together slowly, so I wouldn't fall on my face and ruin everything. Halfway down the trail, we saw Aiden running toward us.

"I couldn't wait any longer, Mommy! Sorry!" He ran into the center of us, and we both hugged him. Then he stood between us, took our hands, and we proceeded down the trail. I felt grateful that we were farther than the halfway I expected, which was a good thing, because Aiden didn't keep me as upright as Billy had. But we got to the bottom safely, entered the car, and buckled up.

"Where to now, *navigator*?" asked Billy as he pulled out into traffic.

"Food!" Aiden said. "Go left at the light. There are lots of restaurants down there."

"Not as many as uptown. Do y'all want to go back there?" Where Billy, who was from Massachusetts, had picked up "y'all" from was beyond me.

"No, let's head out of town. Aiden's right. There are restaurants down that way. Besides, Hugo and I probably won't be able to eat much wherever we go, anyway."

"How about a breakfast place?" I asked. "You can have breakfast, can't you? We can look for a place that serves breakfast all day."

Hugo nodded. "That's fine. Martha doesn't have to follow the keto diet like I do. She's doing it to help me stay on it."

"As it should be," said Martha.

The light turned green, and Billy made the left turn and joined the traffic. "Everybody look for a restaurant that might serve breakfast all day."

"What would that look like?" I asked.

"Don't ask me! Ask them!" Billy nodded to Hugo.

Hugo laughed. "Hard to say. Let's look around and see what we come up with."

"We can try someplace, and if it doesn't work out, try someplace else. No big deal. We're not on a time schedule."

"We have to be home before tomorrow," said Aiden.

"Yes, that's true," I agreed. On the way to Martha's before breakfast this morning, Billy had told me there was a memorial service followed by a reception for Virginia Pennington tomorrow. The public wasn't invited to the memorial service, but the reception was open to the public to pay their respects. Billy was going, and I would tag along.

"Hey!" said Aiden. "Look at that! Sheriff Daddy! Turn in here! Quick!"

Aiden pointed to a small shopping mall on the right-hand side. And there, between a tropical fish store and yet another crystal shop was a small restaurant called Keto Kafe. They must have been to Rutledge and copied Rutledge Koffee Korner Kafe!

"Well done, Aiden! Well done!" said Hugo.

Aiden straightened up in the seat beside me and stuck out his little seven-year-old chest. "Thank you, Grampy!"

Billy slowed the car and pulled into the driveway of the shopping mall. He drove up one aisle of cars and down another. It was busy.

"We don't mind walking, Billy. Hugo needs his exercise, anyway."

"What do you mean 'Hugo needs'? Doesn't Martha need exercise as well?" He smiled at her lovingly. I had known the two of them for nearly a year, and had even lived at their bed and breakfast for a couple of months before I had my house, and in all that time, I had never heard cross words spoken between them. The light of love shone in their eyes each time they looked at each other. I hoped Billy and I could keep our love alive like that.

Billy pulled into a spot about halfway down the aisle of parked cars. We got out of the car and walked to the door of Keto Kafe. The "o" in keto was a fat red tomato, and the glass on the front windows was covered with lavishly drawn egg, cheese, and meat dishes. They made me hungry. Billy opened the door, and we all walked in.

Inside was a white tile floor and pale lavender walls. On the walls were poster-size photographs of the different meals offered there. They all looked good.

After taking care of my personal needs, I met everyone at the table. When Aiden saw me sit down, he held up his menu. "They have lots of good food here that I can eat, Mom!"

"You didn't think you could eat anything here, Aiden?" asked Martha.

He shrugged. "I wasn't sure. I don't know what keto is. It might have been gross."

"Remember that keto meal you had at our house?" asked Hugo.

"Oh, yeah!" said Aiden. "That was keto, too, wasn't it? I loved that!"

"Well, there ya go," said Hugo. "Eat a dog, eat a cat! Just make sure you're eating fat!"

"That's gross, Grampy. Now I miss Bingo." Aiden put the menu down, crossed his arms, and looked sad. Bingo couldn't go with us today because he would have had to spend too much time in the car alone. But he was fine at our house. Billy had installed a dog door, so Bingo could go out into the fenced yard any time he wanted.

"Oh, Aiden. You know he doesn't mean it," said Martha.

"I know. I still miss him."

"Do you know what you want to eat, Aiden?" I asked.

"Yeah. Burger and fries."

"Where's that?" I asked. "I didn't think they'd have fries here."

"They don't," said Billy. "He's trying to pull one over on you."

"Is that true, Aiden?" When Aiden laughed, I shook my head. "Smart aleck kid."

The menus were clean and white and looked almost new. Maybe the place had just opened, but it was already popular, with most of the tables filled. The waitress, dressed in a white apron with Keto Kafe on the front with the same fat, red tomato as the "o," came over and we ordered. She wrote everything down with a pencil she retrieved from behind her ear. Aiden ordered a lettuce-wrapped bacon cheeseburger with jalapeño poppers; Billy ordered the same thing, so I ordered it, too. Hugo ordered a burrito-less burrito bowl, and Martha ordered a chef's salad.

When the waitress walked away, still writing down our order, Martha spoke. "Okay, you two. No wedding in the fancy chapel. What next did you have in mind?" Before we answered, she added, "Too bad your house isn't finished yet, Billy."

She was talking about the house Billy had bought on Hillside Terrace—the exclusive street of mostly mansions where I grew up. His house was the smallest on the block and was a mess when he bought it, but now, he was almost finished with the renovation—not close enough to get married there, though.

"Well, I wanted her to marry me up on Airport Mesa just now, but she turned me down."

I looked at him, surprised. "I thought you were just kidding."

"I don't kid about such important things."

"But then I couldn't have been there!" said Aiden.

"You were there, kiddo!" said Billy.

Martha, looking uncomfortable, said, "Well, you two think about it, and let us know. If we come up with anything, we'll let you know."

"How about at the historical society?" asked Aiden.

"No," I said, shaking my head. "Too many murders there—especially with the last one so recent."

"Let's talk about something more appetizing," said Hugo. "Like eating dogs and cats!"

Aiden picked up his head, shocked, and then growled at Hugo. When Hugo just laughed, Aiden snapped his teeth at him, like he was biting.

"Now, children," said Martha. We all laughed, and the waitress brought our order and set it on the table.

CHAPTER TWENTY-FOUR

THE FOOD WAS delicious—keto or no—and everyone cleaned their plates, even Aiden. He enjoyed his meal so much, he wanted to order it again to take home with him. We trudged out to the car with our bellies full, and it was no surprise that everyone in the back seat— Martha, Aiden, and I—fell asleep on the way home. Hugo stayed awake to talk to Billy.

I woke up when we crossed the bridge into Rutledge, but Martha and Aiden still slept. A minute later, Billy pulled into Martha and Hugo's driveway. He turned around to look at Aiden. "He's asleep, huh? I'll get him." Martha woke up when she heard Billy's voice, but Aiden kept sleeping. He'd had a very hard day!

Hugo came around and put his arm around Martha when she got out of the car. Billy handed Hugo the keys to the Cadillac and reached in to get Aiden. I unfastened Aiden's seat belt, and Billy pulled him out.

"Hey, little pard. You must have had a hard day." Aiden nodded and put his head on Billy's shoulder. "Lorry, how about if you drive the truck home, and I'll sit in the back with Aiden?"

"I can't drive a truck in these!" I pointed to my heels.

"Oh, Lorry." Billy frowned, opened the back door of his truck, and carefully slid Aiden inside.

"Sorry!" I climbed in the back and fastened my seat belt and Aiden's. He fell onto my shoulder, and I heard him softly snoring.

Billy got in the truck, started it, and drove us home without saying a word. If he was mad, let him be. It wasn't just that I had heels on. It was that I had never driven a big truck like this before, and I was apprehensive.

When we pulled in front of my house, before getting out of the truck, Billy looked at me in the rearview mirror. "You've never driven a truck before, have you?" When I shook my head, he said, "Were you afraid to try?" I nodded my head, and he continued, "Why didn't you just say so? That's more understandable than your shoes!" He turned around and reached back to me. "I'm sorry I got impatient with you. I should have known. Sorry."

He got out of the truck, leaned into the back, and pulled Aiden out. Aiden was starting to wake up. "I can walk, Sheriff Billy."

"Let me carry you inside, little pard. We're almost there."

Hurrying, I got to the front door before Billy and held it open for him. Bingo attacked us at the door. He jumped on Billy trying to reach Aiden, and he jumped on me. He couldn't stop whining or wagging his tail. Clearly, he was not a dog who was left home alone often.

Billy carried Aiden directly into his bedroom, with Aiden complaining all the way. "I'm not ready to go to sleep. It's too early!" Aiden protested.

118

Billy put him on the bed and began pulling his sweatshirt over his head. I stood beside the bed and watched.

"Aiden, if you don't want to go to sleep yet, that's fine. But how about if you just lay in bed and read? That's okay, isn't it?"

"All right," he said reluctantly.

We left him in his bed with his books beside him, the light on beside his bed, and Bingo curled up next to him. Billy and I made ourselves comfortable on the couch. We talked about the day and how neither of us was disappointed that we couldn't get married in the fancy chapel.

"But where should we get married?" I asked.

Billy turned toward me with a serious expression and said, "I don't care. I just want to marry you. We could get married in the sewer for all I care."

He was so serious, I had to lighten the mood. So I said, "Gro-oss! I can't imagine what that would do to my heels."

That worked. We laughed and then talked about our day and how pretty the red rocks of Sedona were, my aborted hike to Bell Rock, and our trip up to Airport Mesa. He didn't mention what he said to me up there about getting married, and I was glad. I had no doubt about wanting to marry Billy, but I wasn't sure what he meant up there by "right here, right now," because I wanted something more traditional—not necessarily in a church, probably not in a church—but at least someone there to say "I now pronounce you husband and wife." That wasn't too much to ask.

Then we talked about Martha and Hugo and how well they got along, and how we wanted our relationship to go that same way. Billy said, "No, not how much we want that. It will be *exactly* what we do!" Then he kissed me and said he needed to get home so he could get an early start on investigating Virginia Pennington's murder. I wanted to tell him about what I realized while I was in —or around—the vortex, but I was so tired, I forgot. Billy kissed me good night, and I felt like life couldn't get much sweeter. I loved a wonderful man, and he loved me, we were to be married soon, and we had Aiden and Bingo, and life was awesome. Little did I know what would happen in the not too distant future.

CHAPTER TWENTY-FIVE

BILLY CAME OVER for breakfast at nine o'clock. It was Sunday, pancake day. I served blackberry pancakes and real maple syrup. I wasn't much into health foods, and I wouldn't call maple syrup a health food, but the *fake* maple syrup was just high fructose corn syrup, and I knew that wasn't good for anybody. Why did I know that it wasn't good? Aiden told me. And I believed him. He researched and read extensively on anything that interested him, and sometime in the recent past, he became interested in sugar. They must have been studying nutrition in school, although one never knew where Aiden got his ideas for his reading.

"Sheriff Daddy, when you get back, can we practice karate?"

Billy kept eating and didn't look up.

"Sheriff Da—oh—Sheriff Billy? When you get back, can we practice karate?"

Aiden looked so sad when he corrected himself that Billy reached out and put a hand on his shoulder. "Son, you can call me that soon enough, okay? Just not yet. Yesterday was special. Until your mother and I are officially married, it's not *proper*, okay?" Billy was always clear about doing the *right thing*. Aiden looked down at his pancakes and nodded his head. So Billy squeezed his shoulder and said, "And we can definitely practice karate when we get home, but prepare yourself to get clobbered!"

Aiden finally smiled, shook his head, and said, "I don't think so!" They both laughed, and the tension was broken. Aiden and Billy had been taking karate lessons together, Aiden on Wednesday in the children's class, and Billy on Thursday.

We talked about light topics while we finished eating, and then the four of us—Bingo could go with us today—loaded ourselves into Billy's truck, with Aiden and Bingo in the back. Billy dropped Aiden off at his best friend Lily's house—Lily was the daughter of my cousin Kasey and her husband John—and we drove to the Rutledge Community Church.

I hadn't been to the large, brown brick building with arched stained glass windows since the Celebration of Life I attended for the first dead body I found at the Rutledge Historical Society. Now I was back at the church for another dead body. Color me jinxed? Gosh, I hope not.

Billy would normally take my hand or arm as we walked, but he considered this sheriff business, so we had to show more decorum. Or something. He even wore his sheriff clothes today: dark brown slacks, light brown shirt, a bolo tie, and cowboy boots. He left his hat in the truck. I wore a simple black silk skirt and black silk blouse. Although I wasn't even sure they did that anymore, I figured it wouldn't be out of place, either.

The doors to the chapel were closed, and a large sign with dark blue letters said *Pennington Reception* with a big arrow pointing to the left. To the right of the sign was another large sign that said *Cartwright Celebration of Life* with a big arrow to the right. That's where the previous Celebration of Life had been. Unfortunately, that was also where the kitchen was. Although I had just eaten my delicious blackberry pancakes, eating food at one of these affairs always took the edge off.

We walked down the hallway, bereft of religious pictures on the wall, because the church served all religions in town, and came to a door with a sign that said *Use Other Door.* We continued down the hallway hearing voices from within. Walking in, I saw that it was a smaller room than the other one, but lucky for me, there were two tables of cold cuts and other hors d'oeuvres that looked delicious even from the doorway.

There weren't many people milling around, fewer than ten, including me and Billy. There were several people at the other end of the room, including Jacqueline Pennington. When we walked in, she noticed and smiled. Billy walked her way as she walked his. I stood just inside the door and looked around the room. It was more festive than the other room, but not by much. It had a flowered wallpaper in muted tones with matching curtains over the windows that lined the opposite wall. The off-white tiles on the floor looked new.

I glanced over at Billy and Jacqueline. She was introducing him not to the group she was with, but to two older men, one distinguished looking gentleman wearing an expensive black suit with a dark blue tie, and the other in an equally expensive black suit and a gray tie. The younger one resembled the older one, so

123

perhaps they were brothers. Billy shook hands with them both, and Jacqueline left them alone and walked my way. There was another man alone, also wearing a black suit, but he was alone at the refreshment table.

"Hello, Lorry," she said as she reached me. "Did you come to see who of the guests is the guilty one?"

"Well, I've realized that it's not you."

"Thank you," she said and did a mock curtsy. "My mother could be a pain, but I loved her despite it and would never kill her. She was already too close to death with her emphysema. I don't think she would have lasted much longer, regardless. She was having more and more trouble breathing."

"I'm sorry, Jacqueline. Can I ask you an inappropriate question?"

"As long as you've said you don't think I did it, go ahead!"

"Did your mother have any life insurance?"

Jacqueline laughed. "Lorry, I'd been supporting her for more years than I could count. Why would I pay for life insurance when I'd be the one getting the settlement? She was expensive enough as it was—she had to have the best of everything. Of course, so do I, so I couldn't blame her." She looked me up and down. "And I see you do, too."

That made me laugh. "You know, I left my first husband nearly a year ago, and we pretty much had nothing. But I made sure that the clothes I wore were top of the line. I'd eat beans every day, but my clothes had to be expensive." I don't know why I was telling her this, but she made me feel at home, and like the first time we talked, I *liked* her.

"Your first husband? It looked like you and Sheriff Madrigal came in together. Are you two an item?"

I might have blushed, but I wouldn't admit to it. "He's my fiancé. And a much better man than my first husband—no comparison, really. The first guy was a jerk."

Jacqueline looked thoughtful and then waved her hand around the room. Billy still talked to the two men, the people Jacqueline had been talking to were still clustered together, and the single man stayed at the refreshment table, but he was looking right at us. "So do you see anybody here who looks like a likely suspect?"

Smiling, I shook my head. "I have no idea. Billy has told me before that the murderer coming to the funeral is a cliché better left to books and movies." I glanced around at the people again. "But as long as you asked, who are these people?"

She smiled, blinked her eyes in a knowing manner, and said, "That group of people I was with are coworkers. They only came to support me. The two men I introduced Sheriff Madrigal to are my uncle—great uncle, really—Howard Strong and his son Leonard Strong."

"Oh, so Howard Strong is the one married to—" but I didn't get to finish.

"I don't know who that man at the refreshment table is." She nodded her head toward the man. "The memorial service was closed to the public, but he came in anyway and sat at the back. And when he came in here, he didn't introduce himself."

At that minute, Billy finished talking to the elder and younger Strong—father and son, not brothers as I had thought—and approached the refreshment table. When the single man saw him approaching, he slid out the door. Billy was casual about it; he picked up a piece of cheese, stuck it into his mouth, and then followed the man out the door. But a minute later, I heard a car tearing out of the parking lot.

"That was odd," said Jacqueline.

"Very. And you don't know who he was. That's weird."

She nodded. "I know. I know."

"Hey, can you introduce me to your uncle?"

"Sure. Come on."

We walked over to the two men. The older one smiled, the other one looked annoyed.

"Lorry Lockharte, I'd like you to meet my uncle, Howard Strong, and his son, Leonard. Uncle Howard, Leonard, I'd like you to meet my friend, Lorry Lockharte." Then she nodded, said, "Bye, Lorry," and walked back to her coworkers.

Leonard looked sixty years old, so his father, Howard Strong, must have been in his eighties. But he stood straight and true, and when I saw him walking earlier, he walked like a young man with a spring to his step. Although both men wore expensive suits and shoes, Howard's patent leather shoes looked like they cost more than my car.

Leonard waved and said, "Hi" in a fashion I would have to call juvenile. But Howard took my hand, shook it lightly and said, "I'm charmed, Lorry. Is that Lorry Lockharte of the Rutledge Lockhartes?"

"Yes," I replied. "That's me."

"Do you live in town? Have a business in town?" While he was talking, Leonard walked over to the refreshment table and didn't return.

126

"Yes and no. I live here, but I work at the Rutledge Historical Society."

"Oh, yes, where my poor niece met her demise."

At first, I didn't know who he was talking about. But then I realized that the old woman who looked so much older than he did, Virginia Pennington, was his niece. "Yes, that she did."

"The whole thing was so sad. The sheriff told me he hasn't gotten too far on the case yet." He shrugged. "No fingerprints or anything."

"No, nothing like that."

"And what was she even doing there? I know she was in failing health. I would have thought Jacqueline would have kept her at home."

"She was looking at the new exhibit." It made me think he didn't know her very well if he didn't know how obsessed she was with the murder like Jacqueline had told me.

He smiled at me, a flirty smile. "I'll have to come visit you there and see the exhibit for myself."

I wasn't going to tell him that Billy was my boyfriend. I hated women who identified themselves through their husband's accomplishments. So instead I replied, "I think you'll find it interesting." I looked around the room, because the one I really wanted to talk to was his wife, but Jacqueline hadn't pointed her out. "Is your wife here?"

He glanced around at his son standing at the refreshment table and said quietly, "Oh, no, she's gone."

"Oh, I'm sorry. I didn't know."

He reached for my hand again, shook it softly, and said, "It was a real pleasure meeting you, Lorry, and I hope to see you again."

"Nice meeting you, as well." Then I saw Billy in the window of the door he had disappeared out of, and he was motioning for me to come out. So I glanced again around the room, spotted Jacqueline, waved to her, and then slipped out the door to join Billy.

CHAPTER TWENTY-SIX

WE WALKED TO the truck together without speaking. After we were both inside, I said, "I know you didn't catch that man. Did you get his license?"

"No chance. He was already halfway down the street by the time I left the building. But I noticed that he had out-of-state plates on his car." He looked at me and smiled. "And in case you're wondering, I didn't go after him right away, because it didn't seem proper to chase someone out of a church. That wouldn't have been respectful."

I smiled back at him. "I figured that, Billy. I wasn't wondering!"

He put his hand on my knee and quickly glanced at me and then back at the road. "So do I have to worry about you leaving me for Mr. Strong?"

"Oh, probably not. He doesn't look or act it, but he's in his mid-eighties. I have to draw the line at seventy." Billy took his hand away and laughed. If Howard Strong was seventy, he would still be more than twice my age, and I wasn't into that old man stuff—never was, and never understood women who were. But Billy was kidding, anyway. I think.

"So did you see anyone there besides the guy who ran out who could be a suspect?" I asked.

Billy shook his head. "Hard to tell. Nobody jumped out at me, but killers rarely do." Stopped at a stop sign, he looked at me. "You? Did you see anyone that *you* suspected?"

"Now you're just teasing me!" I crossed my arms and pretended to pout. Or maybe it was real. Half the time I wasn't even sure myself.

"You do jump to conclusions faster than a jack-in-the-box, Lorry." He smiled at me, which lessened the insult but didn't eliminate it. But, I had to admit, it was true.

"Yes, but sometimes I'm right! You have to admit that!"

He chuckled and nodded. "Yes, I admit that." Billy pulled the truck over to the curb at Lily's house. "Here we are."

Aiden must have been waiting at the window, because the front door flew open and Aiden ran to the truck. He climbed into the seat, slammed the door, and before he even had his seat belt on, he asked, "So did you see the murderer?" Bingo jumped into his lap and licked his face.

We both laughed. "It was a reception for the woman who was murdered, Aiden. That's all. We went to pay our respects."

"Oh, I thought this was to interview potential bad guys and girls."

"So you think it could have been a woman, huh, Aiden?" I turned around to look at him.

He crossed his arms in front of his chest and said, "Never underestimate the power of a woman!"

Billy laughed so hard, the truck jerked forward. I hiccuped and was glad I didn't have time for any cold cuts. Aiden sat there with his arms still crossed and looked stoic. "So, Sheriff Billy, are we still going to practice karate when we get home?"

"Of course we are, Aiden! You know I'm a man of my word!"

"Okay," Aiden said and uncrossed his arms.

When we arrived home, Aiden and Bingo ran to the front door. Billy put his arm around me, hugged me to him, and kissed me on the top of the head. "You know I love you, even though you jump to conclusions." Before I had a chance to stand up for myself, he added, "And yes, like I said before, sometimes you're right."

Billy unlocked the front door, while Aiden jumped up and down holding his arm in karate striking pose and saying, "Hurry up! Karate! Karate! Karate!"

"Sorry, Aiden, you have to wait. I have to fix lunch first."

"I already ate at Lily's! Come on! Come on! Come on!" He grabbed Billy's hand and tried to pull him forward, but Billy, all six feet four of him, didn't budge.

"Let go, Aiden," he said as he removed his hand from Aiden's grasp. "Your mother and I have to eat, even if you don't."

"Okay," Aiden said as he sullenly walked away.

Billy and I walked into the kitchen. "I feel bad," he said, "make something quick."

"How about grilled cheese sandwiches?"

"Perfect!"

"Billy, honestly, we don't have to give him everything he wants exactly when he wants it. I don't want to get him spoiled."

Billy moved his shoulders and neck like he was trying to get something off it. Was this going to be our first child-rearing disagreement? "When I think of the way he was brought up before you started the adoption, I always just want to give him *every*thing," he finally said.

I turned from the refrigerator, with the cheese still in my hand, and looked at him. "We can't always do that, Billy. Spoiling him rotten will be almost as bad as neglecting him."

He sighed. "Yeah, I guess you're right."

I spread butter on the bread like Billy liked it, sliced the cheese and put that on, and put everything into the oven. It wasn't exactly grilled, but that's what we called it. We were both so hungry that we scarfed them right down when they were ready. A few minutes later, I was sitting in the living room watching Billy and Aiden start their match.

Aiden had put on his gi—that's his karate uniform— which consisted of a loose white cotton top and loose white cotton trousers. Fastened around his waist was his yellow obi, a wide, thick belt made from cotton. Billy was shirtless and had on a pair of sweatpants that he kept here for just such an occasion. That happened after Aiden had talked him into a karate match and Billy split his good work pants right in the crotch. Most karate pants had an extra piece sewn into the crotch to enable easier and freer movement for kicking.

The reason Aiden had been so intent on practicing his karate was because soon would be his test for orange belt. Billy was testing, too, but he wasn't as concerned about it as Aiden. One, because the only reason he wanted to get orange was to keep up with Aiden, and two, because Aiden didn't have the confidence because he hadn't practiced karate the whole time he was recovering from his injury. Although that wasn't exactly true. I had caught him secretly practicing in his room, even though he wasn't supposed to. It looked innocent enough to me—him practicing alone—and so I didn't stop it.

Billy and Aiden practiced for more than an hour. I watched briefly and then got a book to read. At the end, they wanted me to time their match. During the ninety seconds, each one would call out when they got a point, and there was only one argument when Aiden thought he deserved one and Billy didn't. But mostly, it was all good fun.

Aiden won the match—just like he always did. Even after his injury and inability to practice, he was still better than Billy. Aiden confided in me that he had read about an experiment where guys either practiced basketball every day for an hour or else *thought* about practicing basketball every day for an hour. At the end of the experiment, the *thinking* group had improved just as much as the *doing* group. And Aiden had spent at least an hour of each day practicing his karate in his mind. And it showed.

When they finished, I made lemonade, and the two of them talked about the good moves of the other. Although Aiden won, he always told Billy about how effective some of his moves were. I liked that about Aiden. It wasn't something I taught him, it was something he was—a kind human being. I liked that.

We watched another animal documentary, which Aiden loved. Billy and I enjoyed the animal documentaries, too, but not as much as Aiden. This one was about beavers building dams. It showed some cool underwater videos of the little guys being, you know, busy as beavers!

When we turned off the television, it was almost time for dinner. "How about pizza?" I suggested. I hadn't thought about dinner and didn't have much in the house. There were no more leftovers, and besides, it had been a long weekend and I was tired.

"No, I'm tired of pizza," said Aiden. He sat on the couch in between me and Billy.

"Tired of pizza?" I asked and chuckled. "Are you sick?" I put my hand on his forehead, and he pushed it away.

"Tired of pizza?" asked Billy. "I know what we can do about that!" He began tickling Aiden, and Aiden laughed.

After a minute of the tickling and laughing going on, Aiden said, "Stop, please," and Billy immediately left him alone.

I was old enough to know people who had been tortured by tickling when they were children, and I would not have any part in that. I liked to tickle Aiden, too, but we made the "stop" rule early on. Although I had never told Billy about Aiden and my agreement about tickling, the first time Aiden said *stop* to him, Billy immediately stopped. It was one of the things I liked about Billy. He listened.

"Okay, what do you have in mind then? Takeout?"

"I was thinking about that dinner we had at Grammy and Grampy's—spaghetti pie."

Billy looked at me over Aiden's head and raised his eyebrows. He knew how tired I was. "Are you sure you wouldn't rather have some Chinese takeout?"

"No, Sheriff Billy, I'd really like spaghetti pie."

I took a breath, sighed, and said, "All right, I can do it. I'll call Martha for the recipe, but you two have to do the shopping."

"That sounds fair," said Billy. "You up for it, little pard?"

"Yeah! Spaghetti pie! And when we get back, I'll even help you cook!"

I got on the phone with Martha, and she put Hugo on the line, because he was the cook of the family. He gave me the recipe, and I wrote it all down. Then he insisted on giving me the chocolate cheesecake pie recipe, too. He said it complements the dinner and that Aiden loved it. Saying thank you, I didn't tell him how much I loved the chocolate cheesecake pie, too. I sent the boys off with the list, took my clothes off, got on the bed in my robe, and fell asleep.

Waking up to the smell of something cooking in the kitchen, I blinked and tried to get my bearings. You know that feeling when you take a nap in the middle of the day and you wake up disoriented? Well, color me disoriented. But I stretched and realized where and who I was, and I got dressed in a dark blue skirt with a light blue blouse. It wasn't good enough anymore to wear out, but it was still fine for inside the house. And it cost a fortune—before I had a fortune—so I wasn't willing to part with it. Besides, I looked good in it. Billy had mentioned that more than once, bless his heart.

"Hello, boys," I said as I walked into the kitchen. "Thanks for getting started. Now where are we?"

"We cooked the squash for fifteen minutes, then I took it out and cut it, and just put it back in to bake."

"And I shredded the cheese!" said Aiden.

"Good job! Let me get the hamburger started." Taking the hamburger out of the refrigerator, I said, "Billy, before I forget, I wanted to tell you that I think you should remove that gun from the exhibit. I know the Lexan is strong, but still, whoever killed the woman and tried to get into the exhibit will probably try again. I'm surprised he or she hasn't already tried."

"Good idea. I've been thinking the same thing. Remind me after dinner, will you? Right now my stomach is shouting louder than my brain!"

With everyone helping, dinner was on the table in no time, and the chocolate cheesecake pie was in the oven tempting us with its delicious aroma. Everyone agreed that it was a great dinner and even better dessert. We all had full and happy tummies when we went to sleep that night.

Before he left, Billy kissed me goodbye at the door. But I forgot to remind him about the gun, and the result was almost disastrous.

CHAPTER TWENTY-SEVEN

I WOKE UP early that morning and had no inkling of the dread and double dread that lay before me. Snow dripped from the sky. It was that temperature outside too warm for snow and yet too cold for rain. When Bingo came in from doing his business—which he concluded as fast as he could—he was covered with the wet clumps. Taking a towel from the linen closet in the bathroom, I dried him off, while he wiggled and smiled from under the towel.

I shook my finger at Bingo so he wouldn't go in and wake Aiden. He might or might not have understood me, but he followed me into the living room where I planned to read. Aiden often got up early and read in bed, but when I peeked in his room, he was still sleeping.

When it was time, I called from the living room for Aiden to get up and get ready. Sometimes—no usually— he would read in bed before school in the morning. I would pretend I didn't know, and he would pretend that I didn't know, and all was well. Not that I minded him reading in the morning, but it was just our routine, and we stuck to it.

I fixed him his cereal and juice. He liked the juice with pulp in it, and although I originally didn't, I learned to like it, too. Aiden said it was healthier, and with all the reading he did, I believed him. Then I put two eggs on to soft boil and while I was waiting, I made his lunch. He liked a salami sandwich with mustard on one piece of bread—whole wheat, of course—and mayonnaise on the other piece of bread. Then I put in a large chunk of cucumber and two Oreo cookies.

When Aiden came in, he sat at the table, poured his milk onto the cereal, and said, "Mommy? Can I have chocolate cheesecake pie for dessert instead of Oreos today? Pl-ease?" He drew out please into two syllables for effect.

But I didn't fall for it. "Sorry, kiddo, it's too messy."

He started arguing, "No, it isn't—" but I stopped him short by holding up my hand.

"All right, then. You want me to tell you the real reason?" He nodded. I leaned over and put my face two inches from his. "More for me!" Then I laughed an evil sounding laugh, and we both giggled. And contrary to public belief, giggling is not reserved for children. Adults are perfectly capable of it, as well. Aiden liked it when I giggled. I tried not to do it around Billy, so I didn't know what he thought of it.

"Okay, then. *Promise* me you won't have any for lunch today!" Aiden had an arrogant look on his face, like he won. And he had.

Raising my nose into the air, I said, "Fine. Then I'll have double for dinner!"

"Nooooooo!" said Aiden.

And we both giggled again. We had that kind of relationship—playful. He wasn't ever really disrespectful; it was all part of the game.

We finished eating and both of us got dressed. I wore my yellow and black striped dress with yellow heels. You know how they say vertical stripes make you look thinner? I'm here to tell you it doesn't always work. Nope, it doesn't. Aiden wore his standard blue jeans and Van's tennis shoes with a sweatshirt that had a picture of Winnie the Pooh on it.

Although it was still early, I loaded Aiden and Bingo into the car and drove to the historical society. It surprised me to find Billy's sheriff's car in my spot.

"Sheriff Billy!" cried Aiden. "I want to go in and see him! It's still early!"

"Sorry, little man. You saw him before you went to bed last night. Let's get you to school so I can get to work."

"O-kay," said Aiden, disappointed.

It had stopped snow/raining, and the three of us walked in silence the short distance. I kissed him goodbye, waved to Pamela Reilly, and Bingo and I quickly walked back because I was curious why Billy was there so early. Maybe something had broken on the case?

I used my key and opened the back door. Bingo and I walked in heading toward the front. When I noticed that the chain holding the sign that said *No Admittance* was down, I didn't think anything of it because I knew Billy was inside, and besides, we weren't open yet. What did surprise me, though, was when he popped out from behind the exhibit wall holding his gun with his finger on the trigger. It's funny the little details you notice when you feel like your life is in danger. Involuntarily my arms sprang up over my head. "Billy! It's me! Don't shoot!"

Billy spun his gun like a gunfighter—he probably didn't even realize he did it—and slid it into its holster. Then he wrapped his arms around me. "I'm sorry, sweetie. I'm sorry. I didn't mean to aim at you. So sorry." He kissed me on the lips.

"What are you even here for, Billy? Not that I mind, of course, but I'm just wondering why you were hiding behind the exhibit and jumped out at me like I was a common criminal or something."

Billy had a sly smile on his face. "There's *nothin'* common about you, darlin'!"

I gave him a quick peck on the cheek. "Thank you. But you didn't answer my question."

"Remember you told me last night while we were fixing dinner that I should get the gun out of the exhibit?"

"Yes, and I forgot to remind you. Sorry. But—" Suddenly it dawned on me what Billy was doing here.

He nodded. "Yup. Someone tried to break in last night. I got the call just after three." When Billy first had the alarm installed, it had been a silent one. He figured that he could sneak up on whoever broke in and catch them in the act. But after he asked me to marry him, he thought it would be more circumspect to scare them away and try to figure out who it was with forensics.

"You didn't catch him, though."

"No, nor did I catch *her*."

"Point taken."

"So, anyway, can I have the key so I can get the gun out of there and put it someplace safe?"

140

"Sure. Is that why you're still here? Guarding the gun?"

"Exactly. Can I have the key?"

"Sure. It's in Petra's desk. I'll get it." I strolled down the hallway, stopped at Petra's desk, pulled out the key, and hurried back to Billy. "Here it is."

Billy put the key in the lock, pulled out the gun, admired it, checked to make sure it wasn't loaded, stuck it in his pants, locked the cabinet, and handed me back the key.

"Where are you going to put it?" I asked.

He smiled. "Like I told you, someplace *safe*." Then he kissed me again, walked to the back door, and stepped out.

That's how my morning started. The first dread was having a gun pointed at me by my fiancé. It wasn't the first time he had done that, but in all fairness, he wasn't my fiancé back then. And my day only got worse from that gun. Much worse.

CHAPTER TWENTY-EIGHT

AFTER RETURNING THE key to Petra's desk, I sat down at my own and turned on the computer. Now that Martha did her own typing, I didn't receive many emails except cute animal pictures from Petra and chess challenges from her boyfriend, Mason, who lived in Flagstaff. And as suspected, when my email program came up, there was nothing there except what I mentioned above. This time, though, in Mason's email, he said if I didn't want to play, maybe Aiden would. Mason had taught Aiden to play just before Thanksgiving last year. But Aiden, after me giving him free rein to say yay or nay, opted for a new game that Billy bought him called Stone Age. It was his decision to play that instead of chess. Sorry, Mason!

Petra came in looking grim. She didn't even look at me when she walked in and past me.

"Hey, Petra, good morning."

"Yeah," is all she said.

I stood up and walked to her desk. "What's up, Petra? I know it's something. Spill."

"Oh, Lorry. That jerk of a father of mine has started hitting my mom."

"I didn't think he did that," I said. I knew at Thanksgiving he had given her a black eye, but I didn't mention it.

But Petra did. "Ever since Thanksgiving when Mom ate at your house instead of waiting all day for him not to come home, he's been hitting her. Now she's talking about getting a job so she can leave him."

"That sounds like a good idea."

"Yeah, but all she's ever been is a housewife. What could she do? At first, I thought he'd get over the hitting business and things would go back to normal—at least the messed-up normal like it's been. But he's getting worse." She shook her head. "I don't know what to tell Mom, and I don't know what I can do." She looked up at me. "Not your problem, though."

"I'm sorry, Petra. I wish there was something I could do."

She nodded and turned her computer on. Having finished checking my email, I retired up the stairs to work on the scanning. After sitting down at the desk, instead of starting on my work, I started thinking. *I* knew what kind of job Petra's mom could do! I hurried downstairs to run it by Petra.

"Petra, I've got it! How is your mom at housecleaning?"

"Oh! The best! My father used to yell at her if there was one mote of dust on the furniture. She learned quickly to make it perfect. But why do you ask?"

"That's what she can do, Petra! Clean houses! There's money to be made there! And she can start with mine! I'll hire her!"

"Really, Lorry? You'd do that?"

"Of course. I wouldn't mind somebody else to do my cleaning. Have her come in to see me, and we'll set something up."

"That's great, Lorry. Thank you. I'll tell her when I get home tonight." She moved back in front of her computer and without turning around said, "Kindness. From the 1300s, meaning courtesy, noble deeds. Thank you for that, Lorry. Noble deeds, I mean." Then her fingers moved on the keyboard, and she was silent.

Feeling good about myself, I walked back down the hallway to return upstairs, when I thought of something bad. So I slunk back to Petra's desk to ask her something embarrassing. Sometimes doing good deeds is harder than it seems. "Um, I hate to ask this, Petra, but is your mom honest?"

"Oh, Mom is extremely honest. No question about that. But I would recommend locking up any money or jewelry you or Aiden have in drawers or stuck anywhere else in the house. My father will tell her to take it, and to avoid his wrath, she'll take it and give it to him." She shrugged and returned to her computer work. Then she turned back around, dug into her purse, and pulled out a ten and two fives from her wallet. "On second thought, here's some money for you to leave in drawers for her to find *accidentally*. If she doesn't bring any extra home, he'll accuse her of holding back on him. It won't be pretty."

I pushed the money away and said, "I think I can handle that, Petra. No worries."

Returning to my upstairs desk, I sat down, but didn't feel much like scanning documents. So I got out my little notebook and pen and thought again about the old woman's murder. Since someone had tried to come into this building—it had to be for the gun, what else was there of value?—someone, the murderer, was still concerned. So the best place to start would be with the old woman. She had made some comments to me the first time she came in and more comments the other times. I needed to sit there and remember exactly what she said.

I looked around the room. Rocky came over and rubbed against me, which woke up Bingo, who was sleeping at my feet. Rocky jumped into my lap, and Bingo put his two front paws on my lap and licked Rocky in the face. So far, I had remembered nothing. Maybe it was just a waste of time. I might as well go back to scanning. Let Billy handle it and forget about it.

But as I sat there petting Rocky with one hand and Bingo with the other, it started to calm me. And I didn't even sneeze. Then Rocky took a swipe at Bingo and another swipe at me. I dumped him off my lap, Bingo chased him around the corner, and I sat there, remembering what happened when I went to the vortex. So I closed my eyes and took a deep breath. Oh, come on, Lorry, how can you remember a couple of sentences from months back? Pushing through the doubts and my own impatience, I took another deep breath and relaxed.

And it came to me. In my mind, I could recreate exactly what happened. As the old woman walked past me, with Jacqueline following behind, she said, "You're missing two of the suspects up there! One of them is just in the wrong place! Make sure you fix that!"

I took another deep breath and tried to absorb her words and figure out what they meant. My first inclination was to hurry downstairs and look at the exhibit. But since I was doing so well with remembering,

I didn't budge. Then I tried to focus my attention on just a few days ago—the day she had been murdered. Taking another deep breath, I tried to clear my mind and remember.

Visualizing meeting her at the locked door of the historical society, I remembered her yelling at me, and me opening the door for her. She went to the back, and as Jacqueline walked in the front door, the old woman called out, "I *told* you that you're missing two of the suspects!" When Jacqueline escorted her out, as she passed me, she said, "I told you *last time* I was here that you didn't have all the suspects up there! And do you fix it? No!" Then she returned. She thumped her walker down the hallway and yelled at the people in front of the exhibit to get out of the way. The crowd left, leaving her there alone—or so I thought. She called out to me while I was upstairs, "When are you going to fix the rogue's gallery down here? You're missing two suspects—a man and a woman! That gun is not the murder—*You!*" And then she was shot.

Before I had a chance to assimilate the information, Petra called from the front, "Lorry! Someone here to see you!"

CHAPTER TWENTY-NINE

WALKING CAREFULLY DOWN the stairs—I was still shaky from the experience. It was almost as if I could hear the old woman's voice, but since I didn't believe in ghosts, I knew that wasn't it. I guess part of what shocked me was that I had remembered it all so clearly. Then my head started to clear, and I wondered who had come to see me. Sam had mentioned that she might stop in today. It was probably her.

But it wasn't. As I turned the corner into the hallway at the bottom of the stairs, I could see Howard Strong flirting with Petra. Yes, he was flirting. An eighty-something old codger holding her hand and gazing into her eyes. At the same time, I saw that Petra was trying to pull her hand back. It reminded me of my first husband, Eddie, now deceased, who flirted with anyone with a skirt on. Yuck. My opinion of the elegant and debonair Howard Strong just took a nose dive.

When he heard me coming down the hall—I admit that I stomped my feet a little so he could hear me in case he was hard of hearing, which at his age, he probably was—he dropped Petra's hand like he had just discovered he was holding a rattlesnake.

"Lorry," he said, "how nice to see you again." He stretched out his arm, palm up, so I could place my hand oh so gently in his, but instead, I tricked him. I grabbed his hand with a grip like he was a weight-lifter, gave it a quick shake, and then released it before he could play his little patty cake game with me.

"Good to see you, too, Howard." I tried to put a smile on my face and probably succeeded, but no guarantees there. "So, you're here to see the exhibit?"

"Well, I wasn't really that interested, but I had a meeting here in town, and thought that if it gave me a chance to see you again, I'd come take a look."

I was just about to ask him if he had a business in town when he interrupted me.

"Shall we?" He put out his arm for me to slip mine through, and reluctantly, I did. He led me to the back like he knew where he was going. As we walked, I heard the tap tap tap of his patent leather shoes, and it made me wonder if he actually had *taps* on them. Maybe he was a tap dancer in his spare time. Or something.

"You've been here before then?"

"Of course, who hasn't? And it hasn't changed much over the years."

"Here we are," I said as we stood in front of the exhibit. I was going to make some smart aleck comment, but I couldn't think of one fitting the situation.

He looked at the exhibit from one side and then another, up and down, and crossed in front of me— without saying excuse me, I might add—to look in the corner as if something might be hidden there.

"I don't understand. Is this all there is?"

"Um, yeah. What else were you expecting?"

"I had been led to believe—erroneously, I see now—that my picture was up there. And—"

"*Your* picture?" I laughed. "Why? Were you a suspect?" The idea of that made me want to giggle, but I stifled it.

"Of course I wasn't a suspect! I was the attorney of record, Everett's attorney," he puffed his chest up at this, "and I would have gotten him off, too, had he not taken his own life first."

"Oh, that's right. I forgot all about that part. You were the attorney."

"And I had also heard the murder weapon was in here —not that I really want to see it, I don't—but I was just curious."

"Yes, whoever told you that was correct. It was in here. But Billy decided that it wasn't right to have it here. The person who killed the old woman, may have tried to break into the exhibit case, and someone tried to break in to the building last night."

"For goodness sake! Did they catch him?"

"You're assuming it was a man. It might have been a woman. And no, the person was not caught."

"Oh, that's too bad. And it's too bad that something as extraordinary as the murder weapon couldn't be in the exhibit. That would bring the people in, wouldn't it!"

Nodding, I gave him a token smile. I was going to tell him what the old woman had said, but since my opinion of him had dropped, so did my inclination to open my big mouth. So it was a good thing.

"Do you know where the sheriff took the weapon?"

I thought that was a strange question, so I told him what Billy told me. "He said he was going to put it somewhere safe."

"Safe? What does that mean?"

Shrugging, I said, "Who knows? I haven't speculated, but safe to me is a safety deposit box, so maybe there."

Mr. Howard Strong gave the exhibit one more going over and turned to me. "Well, it was very nice seeing you again, Lorry."

He put his hand out again, palm up, and I grabbed it and gave it a quick shake, a little harder than I had intended. "Nice seeing you, too, Howard."

"Goodbye," and he turned and walked down the hallway, stopping at Petra's desk to lean over and probably whisper sweet nothings in her ear.

Standing in place, lest he change his mind and return, I waited until he was out the door before I walked up the hallway.

"Who was that jerk?" asked Petra. "There's nothing worse than a sixty-year-old guy trying to chat me up."

"His name's Howard Strong. He was the attorney in the Pennington murder case. And he's not sixty, he's in his eighties!"

"Even worse!" Petra said and turned back to her computer.

"I know!"

CHAPTER THIRTY

AFTER I CHECKED my email again and found not only nothing of interest, but *nothing*, I returned upstairs. My enthusiasm for the murder had once again waned after the distasteful experience with Howard Strong, so I put the notebook with my notes into the drawer of my desk and set about scanning documents.

Several hours later, I heard Petra call from downstairs, "Lorry! Someone to see you!"

For a second, I thought it might be Howard Strong returning, and I shivered. But Petra would have said something smart alecky if it had been him. Still, I didn't hurry downstairs until I realized that it was probably Sam.

When I turned the corner, it was Sam, and I felt relieved. Howard Strong had begun to remind me of someone else who I had been briefly enthralled with and ended up being so wrong about. But Howard Strong wasn't a killer, he was just a jerk.

"Hi, Sam!"

"Hi, Lorry! Are you ready?"

"Um, ready?"

"Don't you remember? We were going to lunch today!"

I grimaced. "I forgot. Hold on." I walked into Petra's office, and she nodded without turning around.

"Yes, I'll do your job for you. Go ahead."

I laughed at Petra, who could sometimes be cheeky, but never really meant it. She had one of the best hearts of anyone I knew. "Thanks, Petra!" and to Sam, "Let's go!"

"Hey, do you mind a picnic lunch? I brought some food that I thought you might enjoy."

On the floor beside her sat a big woven wooden picnic basket that I hadn't noticed before. "Picnic? Isn't it a little cold for that?"

"We can wear our jackets. Come on, it will be fun!"

"Okay. Where shall we go?" Ah, that was the problem, wasn't it? There were no parks in Rutledge. The closest was fifteen minutes away—more in traffic—in Coyote Moon.

"I was hoping you'd think of someplace," said Sam. "You've lived here longer."

"Petra? You have any ideas of where we can have a picnic lunch around here?"

"The high school? The grammar school?"

Sam and I looked at each other, and both of us shook our heads. "That would be no and no," I said. "Wait a minute." I opened the bottom drawer, pulled out my purse, and then took my cell phone out. Punching up a number, I waited for an answer.

"Hugo? . . . Hi, it's Lorry. . . . Great! How 'bout you? . . . Hey, I was wondering— . . . Yes, I do wonder sometimes, smart guy! Anyway, do you have anyone staying there now? I'm asking because I was hoping Sam and I— . . . No, I'm not leaving Billy. Sam is a female friend! . . . Can Sam and I come over there and have a picnic in the back? Would you mind? . . . Really? . . . Great! Thanks, Hugo! See ya soon!" I looked at Sam. "It's settled. We have somewhere to go. Let's take my car."

"My car is out front, Lorry, and I don't want to schlep this all the way back to yours. I don't even know why I schlepped it out of the car. Do you mind taking mine?"

"Nope, let's go. Bye, Petra." I didn't wait for an answer, because Petra probably wouldn't have given one.

We walked outside to Sam's car, a silver Lexus. It was a beautiful car, but I still loved my RAV4. After stepping into the car and fastening our seat belts, Sam asked, "Okay, where to?"

"Right on Bridge." Sam made the turn, and a minute later, we arrived at the T intersection. "Turn right on Meadowside."

Sam looked at me and said, "I live down there."

"Did you say lived? Yeah, I know. We both did." Hillside Terrace, which was the street if we turned left, was where all the mansions were, and where we both lived when we were in high school.

She looked sheepish. "No, we live there now."

"Seriously? You and Mark and the kids live down there?" I laughed. "That's funny. Whose idea was that?"

"My parents. They still owned the property and thought we should live there and not waste it."

"Here we are. Just pull into the driveway," I told her. "I'm leaving my purse in the car. It's safe here."

"Yeah, good idea. One less thing to schlep. I will, too." She drove into the driveway and turned off the car.

"This is a beautiful old Victorian. It reminds me of your old house."

"I know!"

We got out and Sam lugged—schlepped, in her words —the picnic basket up to the door of the house. Although we could have used the side gate to go directly into the backyard, I wanted to say hello to Hugo and to thank him for letting us do this.

He opened the door dressed in beige dockers and a green button-down shirt. But he had one finger on the top of his head and twirled around saying, "It's time for a picnic, don't you know! It's time for a picnic, I hope it won't snow!" Then he turned to us with a big smile.

"Hugo, this is my good friend, Sam. Sam, this is my good friend, Hugo."

"Howdy do, Sam!" With a big smile, he bent at the waist and bowed low to her.

"Hi, Hugo!"

"Here, let me take that," Hugo said, putting out his hand for the basket. She handed it to him, and he made a big show of almost dropping it and then walking crooked pretending it was too heavy to carry. "I took the liberty of moving the picnic table into the sun for you."

"Thanks, Hugo," I said.

He opened the door for us, followed us out, and placed the picnic basket on the table, where he had spread a red and white checkered table cloth. He bowed again. "At your service, ladies. Let me know if you need anything."

Sam chuckled, and I thanked Hugo again. Before he went into the house, though, he turned around to me.

"How did the spaghetti pie turn out?"

"Oh, Hugo! Sorry I forgot to thank you for that! It was absolutely delicious—not as good as yours, of course —but everybody loved it! And the chocolate cheesecake pie for dessert was wonderful. Thanks so much for the recipes!" He just smiled and walked inside.

Sam and I had just finished laying everything out on the table when Hugo returned with a pitcher of pink lemonade and two glasses. "Enjoy!" And he disappeared into the house.

"He's wonderful," said Sam.

"Yeah, he's my boss's husband. They're both great. Aiden calls them Grammy and Grampy."

The yard looked the same as it always did. There were perennials planted all over, so there were almost always some blooms in the yard. At the back, there was a tall fence made of redwood. There was lawn which was now brown with the winter, and a few good size juniper trees.

Sam and I chitchatted for the next hour about old times, new times, and not so new times. It was all too boring for your sensitive ears, so I won't go into it. And then when I mentioned what had happened that morning with Howard Strong and Petra, the conversation got more interesting.

"He's that attorney from Coyote Moon, isn't he? He must be old by now."

"Yes, he did practice in Coyote Moon, and now he's in his eighties. You know of him?"

She shook her head. "That guy is a real gonif; I know that."

"Interpretation, please," I said. "Although it doesn't sound good. He claimed he was a good lawyer." Sam's use of Yiddish so much in her speech usually threw me, although I was learning some of the words she used more often. She claimed that a lot of those words had made the transition to informal English.

"You're right, not good. Dishonest," she said. "Although, I wouldn't call him a bad lawyer. My parents went up against him for something—and they had a good lawyer—but Strong pulled some shenanigans and my parents lost the suit. It was a long time ago, but I think it had something to do with a contractor who didn't fulfill his obligations. But I do remember Strong was a jerk."

Glancing at my watch, I jumped up. "Oh, Sam! I've got to get back. We've been here more than an hour!" I stuck my head in the door, thanked Hugo, and after everything was packed back up in the picnic basket, we exited through the side gate to the driveway.

Sam dropped me off in the front, and I was surprised to see Billy's car parked out front. I walked in, and he was pacing back and forth down the hallway. When he heard the door open, he rushed over to me.

He took my hands and looked at me with a concerned expression on his face. "Lorry! I've been calling you for an hour, why didn't you answer?"

I frowned. "Oops, sorry, I left my purse in the car and never checked it. Why? What's up?"

Still holding my hands, he said, "I really need to talk —" Glancing out the window, he added, "Listen, I've got to run now. I love you." He kissed me on the lips and slipped out the door.

"He's been here for more than an hour waiting for you, Lorry," Petra said.

Before I could answer, I looked out the window to see a tall, thin woman smile at Billy and put out her arms to him. They hugged, and he kissed her on the lips. And then they walked down the street.

I rushed into Petra's office barely able to speak. "Petra!" I said in a panic. "Billy just hugged and kissed some woman on the lips and walked off with her!"

Petra didn't seem concerned. "What'd she look like?"

"Tall and thin. Short blond hair, nicely dressed. Pretty."

"Oh, yeah. That's his ex-wife, Cheryl."

CHAPTER THIRTY-ONE

TAKING A STEP back, I grasped the partition that separated our respective offices. "Billy—has—an—ex-wife?"

"Yeah. He never told you? Maybe that's why he's been waiting here for an hour," she said with such nonchalance I could have choked her.

Could have, that is, if I could do more than just stand there holding myself up with the partition. I felt like I was plunging into darkness, and I wasn't sure if I could even stand up anymore.

"Lorry? Are you okay? You look weird. All the blood has drained from your face."

"I'm fine!" I said with as much force as I could muster, which wasn't much. Using the wall to support me, I pivoted so I was facing my desk and then stumbled into my chair and put my head between my legs. I knew what was happening: I was about to faint. And I wasn't going to show that weakness to anyone, especially not Petra, and especially not now.

And my harsh and obnoxious tone mollified her so much that she didn't even come in to check on me, which is why I did it. Sitting there studying the floor until the nauseating feeling passed, I finally raised my head and took a deep breath. Then I inadvertently glanced out the window and saw Billy's car out there, which plunged me into darkness again. I never realized how fascinating the floor of the historical society was until now. Not.

When I recovered enough to sit up again, I made sure not to look out the window. No sense courting disaster. I liked to pretend that I was tough, but there were times— like this one—where I could be as vulnerable as everyone else. Grabbing my purse, I stood up, holding onto the desk. Feeling my feet on the floor, I took a deep breath, and tried to get my bearings. Was I back to myself enough to make my way upstairs? There was no sign of the darkness or the nausea, and I thought I could do it.

I gathered up my courage and my strength, and walked out of my office and past Petra's desk, without so much as a pause. After I passed her, though, I immediately leaned on the wall for support, and then half walked and half pulled myself up by the railing on my way up the stairs. When I got to the top, I sank into my chair to rest.

I also needed to think. My original plan had been to get up here, walk to the back corner, and call my cousin Kasey to pick up Aiden from school. But as I sat in the chair, I thought maybe I wasn't giving Billy enough time. It hadn't been that long, and if this was an innocent reunion, I should give him the ole benefit of the doubt and chill. But it was almost three o'clock, so I didn't have time for that.

After waiting a few minutes, I slipped off my shoes, got my cell phone, and headed toward the back corner. I tapped in the number of the cafe next door where Kasey worked and asked for her. When I found out she wasn't working, I tapped in her home number.

"Hi, Kasey. I was wondering if you would mind picking Aiden up from school today and letting him stay over for a couple of nights? . . . No, I'm not whispering. . . . Oh, you can? That's great. Thank you. . . . Yeah, something came up, so I didn't have a chance to talk to him about it. Have him call me tonight, okay? . . . Thanks so much. I'll call Pamela now. Bye."

Then I quickly called Pamela. I felt grateful that she didn't answer. That way, I could just leave a message on her voicemail, and there would be no questions about why I was whispering.

Yes, I was whispering—so Petra wouldn't hear. But she did anyway. When I tiptoed back to my desk in my stocking feet, I heard her say from her office, "So, Lorry, are you talking to yourself now? I thought you were a little young for that, but maybe I'm mistaken."

"Very cute, Petra!" I called down the stairs. She didn't respond.

The notes I wrote down about everything the old woman said were still in the drawer, untouched. But I was in no mood to think about murder right now, except maybe murdering Billy for not telling me this, and I'd throw his ex-wife in, too, just to be fair. Or something.

That thought made me look at my watch. He still hadn't returned from his misadventures, and it was getting later and later. I forced a deep breath in and tried to get involved in the documents I was scanning. There was no use. Every time I heard a sound that could have been the door opening, I leaned over to listen. The door did open once, but it was a family from New York—I could tell by their accents—and Petra directed them to the exhibits. I heard them downstairs, rummaging around, and it ticked me off because they were so loud I couldn't hear if the door opened or not. Finally they left, and I remained in the silence of upstairs.

For the next couple of hours, I listened intently for the front door to open, and for Billy to come in and explain himself, but it never happened. The New York family were the only visitors, and the door never opened again. At five o'clock, I trudged downstairs, locked the front door, turned the sign to *Closed*, and turned off my computer. Billy's car was still out front, and no sign of Billy or the woman.

CHAPTER THIRTY-TWO

WHEN I GOT home, I slipped off my heels and changed clothes. Then I trudged into the kitchen, defrosted something in the microwave that was still in the freezer only because it had too much freezer burn on it to be appetizing. It was tasteless, but it didn't matter. There was only one thing on my mind, and it wasn't food. It was Billy's betrayal. When I finished eating, I wasn't even interested in the chocolate cheesecake pie. That was fine. More for Aiden.

And I wanted so much to turn off my phone so I wouldn't have to listen to its silence, but I knew Aiden would call me at some point—probably after they ate dinner. So I left it on and stared at it. Maybe it needed charging, and that's why it wasn't ringing? No, it had plenty of battery left. That wasn't it, and I knew it. Billy had abandoned me, and I had to live with that. What about Aiden? Losing Billy would kill Aiden. Poor Aiden. I felt so bad for the kid.

The phone rang, but it wasn't Billy. It was from Kasey's house. "Hi, Sweetie. . . .You're welcome! I know how much you like to spend time with Lily. . . . No, I haven't eaten any more chocolate cheesecake pie because I'm saving it for you! . . . Of course that's true. . . . Are you enjoying your time over there? . . . All right. Just two days and then I'll see you. . . . Okay, good. Enjoy every minute, son. . . . I love you. . . . Bye."

I hung up the phone as tears rolled down my face. Thankfully, he had not picked up on my depressive mood. He could usually read me pretty well even when I tried to hide it. But I wouldn't hold it against him, because there was a lot going on at Kasey's house. There was always a lot going on at Kasey's house. While we were on the phone, Lily had thrown a ball at him and knocked the phone out of his hand. No surprise there.

It was no use trying to read because I couldn't concentrate on anything. This was a time when I would have appreciated cable, because I needed some mindless entertainment. Watching the beaver documentary again didn't appeal to me. Bingo jumped up on my lap and licked my tears away. How did I ever do without him? How do people get along without dogs? I never could understand that. When you're feeling down, a dog's wag is like a beacon of light in the darkness. Their ability to give unconditional love surpasses anyone else, including humans. No. Especially humans.

I don't know how long I sat on the couch petting Bingo, but it helped to pass the unbearable time. Finally, I got up and walked to the front window. No Billy and no headlights coming toward the house. Alternating between the window and looking at a blank phone helped me spend thirty more uneventful minutes. When I tired of that, I decided the only thing to do was to go to bed.

Since the only time we left Bingo's dog door open was when we left him alone during the day—because Aiden read somewhere that wild animals might get in—I let Bingo out for his last constitutional before bed, I took off my clothes, changed into my nightgown, turned out the light, and hugged Bingo to me. I felt like I had nothing else. Of course I did, but at that moment, it didn't feel like it. Although I meant to turn off the phone since Aiden had already called, I didn't have the energy to get up and do it. Besides, if Billy wanted to call, he could use the landline, which he usually did anyway. Somehow, I managed to fall asleep.

When I woke up early the next morning, there was still no message or sign of Billy. It practically made me physically ill. But I knew what I had to do. And the first thing was to call the historical society before Petra got in, so I could leave a message and not have to answer her questions. All I said in the message was that I wouldn't be in today. Period. She didn't have to know why. Then I rushed to get dressed in casual clothes—or as casual as I can get with heels on—and went out to start my car and get out of there. I didn't know where I was going, but I had to get out. There was no way I could spend another day wondering if and when Billy would call. My heart couldn't take it.

After I pulled to the end of the driveway, I figured out where I wanted to go. I didn't want to waste the time going back in the house, but I had to. Rushing back in, I grabbed one of Aiden's spare backpacks and stuffed everything I would need into it. Then I rushed back to the car. If Aiden was going to call, he wouldn't until after they ate dinner. Mornings in Kasey's house were more hectic than relaxed, and he wouldn't have time. So I switched off the phone, which made me smile.

Jumping back into the car, I gave Bingo a pat on the head, and pulled out into the street. While I wanted to drive ninety miles an hour out of town, I didn't think that would be appropriate for someone who didn't want anyone to notice that she was leaving. If I could have, I would have tiptoed past Main Street where the sheriff's station was. Although I couldn't see it from Bridge Street, I still had to resist the urge to look down that direction.

Driving across the bridge onto Broadway in Coyote Moon, I felt like I had won—or at least had gotten something over on someone. Who, I don't know. Billy still had made no effort to call me unless it was in the last two minutes. I was sick at heart, but I had won. Kind of. That had to count for something. And right now, I was riding into the sunset. Well, I guess it was the sunrise, except that I was driving west. Details details. I wiped the tears from my face, tried to pretend they weren't really coming from me, and kept going, away from Rutledge and away from heartbreak.

CHAPTER THIRTY-THREE

I DROVE WEST through Coyote Moon and stopped at the golden arches for breakfast. What I really wanted was pancakes and sausage—isn't that what a person did when they were depressed? Ate sugar?—but I didn't want to have to park and eat. So instead I ordered an Egg McMuffin and hash browns. As I drove, I ate, and then turned south on the highway toward Cottonwood. My tears had dried, and I decided to think of the advantages of Billy going back to his ex-wife. I was rich, I was free, I could do anything I pleased. And I had a great idea: Aiden and I would take a world cruise. It would be perfect! It would be awesome! Oh, who am I kidding? It would be awful without Billy. But awful or not, when I got back home, I would immediately investigate the possibilities.

The highway stretched on and so did my misery. As I approached Cottonwood, I knew I would have to decide on which way to go. Should I go east on 260 toward Camp Verde and then take the interstate south? Or should I take 89A up to Jerome and the twisty road down Mingus Mountain? The scary twisty road. At least for

166

me. But why was it scary? Because I was afraid of going off the edge and dying? Taking a deep breath, I choose 89A up to Jerome. Dying didn't seem like such a bad option at that minute. At the very least, it would take me out of the misery that had plagued me ever since I saw Billy kiss *that woman* on the lips.

The drive up the mountain was pleasant enough, and Jerome was a quaint old mining town now populated with artists and cute shops. As I headed down the mountain, I was driving maybe a little faster than was safe, but as I said, I didn't care. But when I came out of the first turn with a screech of tires, I took a deep breath, slowed down, and reconsidered. What would happen to Aiden? No, I could handle this, and there were always options. Although I didn't know what they were, I knew they were out there. For the rest of the trip down the mountain—crawling along—I decided to plan our world cruise.

When I got to the bottom of Mingus Mountain, I turned right to stay on 89A. After a few miles, I took exit 317 and turned left to stay on 89A. I followed that route through what they called The Dells—these gorgeous rock formations almost ruined by urban sprawl. I admired the view and kept going down the road almost to my destination. Slowing down, I turned left up the steep but brief hill, stopped at the stop sign at the top, turned right and then left into the parking lot of the casino.

There wasn't a parking place close to the door, but I could use the exercise, anyway, so I parked in a spot where I had to walk a short distance. I turned off the engine, and then I couldn't help myself any longer! Grabbing my purse and practically ripping it open, I took out my cell phone and turned it on. When it came on, it's blankness almost threw me into the black darkness again, but I wasn't going to allow that to happen. So I took a deep breath, turned it off, clenched my teeth, and used all the will power that I possessed not to throw it across the parking lot. Instead, I dropped it on the floor. Then I grabbed the backpack and my purse, kissed Bingo and told him I wouldn't be long, and locked the car.

The casino was nothing like the one in Coyote Moon. It was a normal building, elegant even, and tastefully decorated. Since I entered through the hotel entrance, there were none of the blasted slot machine noises, which was great. The area was bright and open with subtle Native American decor. There was a beautiful statue of a Native American woman teaching her daughter to make baskets. To the right was the front desk.

"Can I get a day pass for the pool?"

"Sure. Fifteen dollars." She was dressed in a business suit and looked like a professional. This casino was much different from the one in Coyote Moon.

I handed her a ten and a five, and she handed me one of those magnetic cards. "Where's the pool?"

She pointed to a door across the room. I walked over there, stuck the key card into the slot, waited for the green light to appear, and pushed through. The pool was about thirty feet long, and each end was shallow. A sign hung on the wall to my left that said *No Lifeguard*. In front of the sign was a table and chairs, and on the other side of the pool were several lounge chairs. There were no people sunbathing, though, because there was no sun! It was an indoor pool! Hello! I passed by the hot tub that was up a few steps and entered another door. Inside that room were several different kinds of weight machines, a stepper, two treadmills, and two stationary bicycles. An open door was straight ahead, but when I stuck my head in, to the left was a door marked *Janitor*, and a long hallway to the right. I didn't really know where to go.

A man with those earbud earphones was on one of the stationary bicycles, so I walked up to him. He pulled out one of his earbuds and scowled at me.

"This is my first time here," I said. "Where do I go?"

"Through that door and down the hallway," he grumped. Before I had a chance to ask another question —had I another question to ask, which I didn't—he shoved the earbud back into his ear and turned away from me.

Touchy! Touchy! I made my way down the hallway past the doors that said *Men's Dressing Room* and *Treatment A* and *Treatment B*. They did massages here, but today was not the day for that. It would probably relax me, but I felt too stressed out to feel relaxed. Ironic, isn't it? Turning the corner, I saw a shop in front of me that looked like it sold beauty supplies, and to my right was the *Women's Dressing Room*.

Walking inside, I saw two sinks and a big mirror straight ahead of me. To the left was a room marked *Changing Room*. I supposed that was for women who didn't want other women to see their bodies. While I wasn't proud of my overweight self, I wasn't ashamed either. I'd get undressed in front of the lockers. No one was in the room except me, so I stopped in front of the mirror to check myself out. My eyes were not red rimmed like I suspected. But the thought of why they might be red rimmed almost sent me on another crying jag.

169

I walked away from the mirror and put my backpack on the bench by the lockers. Behind me was a picture that at first glance looked like it might be a desert, but at closer inspection, it had a house and barn and windmill on it. Next to that was a big mirror in a wooden frame—just what I needed—another reminder of red rimmed eyes. Directly across from the lockers was the sauna. After turning it on and setting the temperature to hot but not scalding, I sat down, slipped off my shoes, and began getting undressed. When I finished, I pulled on my swimsuit, black of course. Although I wasn't embarrassed of my body, there was no use advertising in front of the male of the species.

Opening one of the lockers, I put everything inside, grabbed a towel from the rack, and walked back out to the pool. There were three old women in the pool talking and fluttering around. They might have been waiting for a water aerobics class. I walked to the shallow end on the far side and went down the stairs. The water was pleasantly warm and took no getting used to. Just the way I liked it. No one knew this about me, but I used to be an excellent swimmer. I was faster than anyone, but I didn't have a lot of endurance. Although I could win short races, I always came in almost last in longer ones. When my mother finally made me choose between chess and swimming, I chose chess.

But it had been a long time since then, and I hadn't swum in years. I started with a slow crawl across the pool and back. The women moved over as I swam by. Then I did a breast stroke across and back. Following that, I did a back stroke and side strokes on both sides. When I finished that, I did them all again and again, until I got to twenty laps. It took me all of ten minutes. I wasn't what I used to be, and at the end of that ten minutes, I was completely out of breath. There was only one thing to do. Grab my towel and get in the hot tub.

After turning the bubbles on for ten minutes, I slid into the hot tub. Oh, my aching bones, that felt good. Actually, it wasn't my bones that were aching but my heart. The hot bubbles seemed to soothe that as well. Conversation from the old women drifted over to where I was. Why do old women always talk about ailments—either theirs or their friends' and relatives'? Hugo and Martha were about the same age as the women in the pool, and they never did that. And I was grateful for that.

When the bubbles ended, I took a deep breath, luxuriated in the hot tub a while longer, and then tore myself away. Although I enjoy the heat, I can't take too much of it. With my towel wrapped around me, I walked through the fitness room, and back into the dressing room. There was still no one in there. After opening the door to the sauna, I walked in, spread my towel on the seat and back of the bench, and sat down. On the bench beside me was a metal container full of water. Inside it was a scoop for throwing the water onto the heater to make a steam bath, but I preferred the plain dry sauna, so I sat back and relaxed.

I heard someone walk into the dressing room and, a short time later, the toilet flush. Then a woman stood in front of the mirror washing her hands. After drying them, she stood in front of the mirror looking at herself one way and then another and patting down her hair. I'm sure she couldn't see me because the door of the sauna was closed, and I was in the corner, but she leaned forward and popped a pimple! I wondered if it was the kind that hit the mirror. Then I realized that I didn't care. She left.

A few minutes later, I realized that sweat was dripping down between my breasts. Then I noticed that my face was sweating, and it was from my eyes. Oh, wait, those were tears. I'd had enough of this. I climbed down, wrapped my towel back around me, turned off the sauna, and found the door to the shower right next to the towel rack. Grabbing two towels on the way in, I dropped my wet towel in the used towel bin. I hung up the two towels on each side of the wall, turned the shower on, and stepped into it. There was a shower curtain, but I didn't pull it closed because I didn't feel like being blocked in. First, I removed and rinsed my bathing suit, and put it on top of one of the clean towels I had brought in with me.

When I finished the shower, I still didn't feel any better. After using both towels to dry off, I noticed that since I hadn't pulled the shower curtain closed, there was water all over the floor. So I took a towel and dried the floor as best I could, and then walked out to the dressing room, dropping the dirty towels into the bin on the way.

I pulled another towel off the rack to sit on, spread it on the bench, pulled my clothes out of my locker, and put them on. Then I wrapped my still wet bathing suit into the towel and plastic bag I had brought from home and put it in the backpack. In front of the mirror, I combed my hair, and as the woman before me, turned this way and that looking at myself. I didn't, however, pop any pimples, because I didn't have any. The next thing on my agenda was to sit in their lobby and read. Although what I really really *really* wanted to do was to walk out to the car and see if Billy had called. Instead, I quelled the urge and walked to the lobby.

CHAPTER THIRTY-FOUR

I WALKED PAST the piano and past the lounge sign, then down the stairs, and across the dance floor. Before I crossed the dance floor—empty in the light of day—I gave a longing look toward the front door. Maybe I could just go check on Bingo, and as long as I was there, I could briefly turn the phone on.

No. Setting my jaw, I walked across the dance floor to a table and chairs. There were several sets of round tables and chairs surrounding the dance floor. The bar was to the left with a television up in the corner, and there was a big screen television on the wall behind two couches facing a coffee table. It was on, and it was loud. Even across the room, I could hear it clearly. And there was no one in the big room but me, but the television still blasted away. I chose the table farthest from it and sat down.

Inside the backpack, I had stuck a book to read, and now I pulled it out and opened it. But I wasn't in the mood for even this good book. It was the third in the series of a time-travel romance, and it was great. When I love a series, I always space them out so I don't go

174

through them all at one time. Currently, I was in the middle of several series. And I liked it that way. Glancing outside through the floor to ceiling glass windows, I saw a beautiful view of the mountains in the distance and urban sprawl in the valley. No way to get around that urban sprawl, is there?

Looking back down at my book, I tried to focus. A man, wearing shiny black shoes, black pants, and a blue checked shirt walked by talking on his cell phone in a loud voice, but it was a welcome interruption. He walked behind me and out into the courtyard, which had a fire pit, tables, and chairs. The expansive view was thrown in for free. He must have been an employee, because as he talked, he went up to the window, and with his free hand scraped something off the glass.

It took me a long time to clear my mind enough to read. All I had left to do was block out the blaring of the television. But after a few sentences, the story gripped me, and I didn't hear the television at all. When I reached the end of the chapter, I looked up. The man had gone, the television still blared, and I dove back into the book. That was the thing for me. Reading was, and always had been, balm for my soul.

After a few chapters I knew it was time to leave and see what, if anything, awaited me on my cell phone. I wondered if Billy had left a message on there that said, "I'm leaving you for my ex-wife. Goodbye and have a nice life." Or would he wait so he could tell me in person? Or was I imagining the whole thing? I did, I knew, get carried away sometimes. And it might be the same for this time, too, except that I had seen him kiss his ex-wife—*on the lips*—right in front of me.

Was I making too much of that? If Eddie wasn't dead, and I ran into him somewhere, would I be happy to see him and kiss him on the lips? I don't think so! No way! But even if I was surmising something without knowing all the facts—which I did have a tendency to do—what really mattered to me was that Billy had, in a way, betrayed me. He had never told me that he had an ex-wife, and I had always assumed he had never been married.

And you know what assume does, but I won't get into that here. How stupid of me to think a gorgeous hunk of a man like Billy would never have been married. The whole thing was my fault. But still, he had never told me. I slipped the book back into the backpack and walked out of the casino.

At the car, Bingo almost wagged himself off the seat he was so happy to see me. I petted him and then let him out to pee in the bushes in front of the car. He jumped back into the car, and I climbed in, reached for the cell phone, and turned it on. Waiting for it to respond was the longest thirty seconds of my life. No messages, but when I checked call history, Billy had called. Once. I guess that shows how much he cares. Once. And no message. And I'm repeating myself, but I had to let it sink in. Starting the car, I pulled out of the parking lot and started heading home, without turning the cell phone off. It wasn't something I could even force myself to do.

When I got to the turnoff for Jerome and Cottonwood, I passed it by. Billy had called. I didn't know what he would say, but I didn't have to torture myself any more by going up the twisty mountain road. He hadn't abandoned me completely. *Completely* being the salient word. So I drove straight, turned left on 69, and then left again on 169 heading up to Interstate 17.

Billy called again, and it was all I could do not to answer the phone. But my stupid willpower held out. He didn't leave a message—probably because he had too much honor to break up with me that way. Sighing, I turned left onto the on-ramp toward Flagstaff and merged with traffic. Right after I took the 287 exit toward Cottonwood, Billy called again. No message again. He had called three times. In my book that meant he cared. Of course, you couldn't always go by my book, because it was often wrong, just like me. But it boosted my spirits that he had made the effort.

Before I got to Cottonwood—which wasn't all that much longer—Billy called again, and this time, he left a message. I resisted the urge to pull over and listen to the message. It was enough that he left it. Well, almost enough. I still felt depressed about the whole situation. I turned up the highway toward Coyote Moon. When I was halfway there, Billy called again and left another message. Things were looking more promising. He wouldn't be calling so often or leaving messages if he was breaking up with me. That made sense, didn't it? I let that sink in, and it made me feel better—whether it was true or not.

Getting off the highway at Coyote Moon, I headed east toward Rutledge on Broadway. Billy called again. Another message. I almost felt elated. Almost. As I drove, I wondered what each message said, but I refused to listen. Not yet, anyway. The time was coming. Traffic was light, so I was on Bridge Street crossing the bridge into Rutledge in no time.

177

Turning left, I drove past the high school and headed toward a parking spot by the river I used to hang out at when I was young—a place to contemplate life. There may have been some necking going on there, but I was never one of the participants.

I parked, took a deep breath, tried to calm myself, and listened to the first message. *Lorry, I'm frantic. Where are you? You're not at home and you're not at work. I'm worried. Please call.* He was frantic, but not frantic enough to say that he loved me. I deleted it, gritted my teeth, and listened to the next one. *Lorry, I love you. I stopped at the historical society and Petra said you almost fainted when you saw me with Cheryl—my ex-wife. I'm so sorry that I didn't tell you earlier. I wanted to yesterday before I met with her. I had planned to introduce you and all, but then you were so late returning from lunch, and she arrived early. And what could I do? Anyway, I'm sorry, and I love you.*

So Petra did know that I had almost fainted. I'll have to give her credit for that. Although, I always seem to underestimate Petra, and Petra always proves me wrong. I should have learned that lesson by now. And Billy loves me. He said it twice. And he apologized. Still, I didn't feel satisfied. He could have said more. I moved on to the third message.

Lorry, I'm so sorry. I talked to Petra again, and she said it probably bothered you that I kissed Cheryl on the lips. She's my ex-wife. It was perfectly innocent. But I won't do that ever again if it bothers you. I want to marry **you**. *No one else. Just you. Lorry, you are the love of my life! Please at least call me and let me know you're safe. All kinds of crazy things are rolling around in my head, and I'm scared.* He sniffled and then went on. I think maybe he was crying. *I love you and I want to marry you and* *there is no woman in the entire universe for me except you! Please forgive me.*

All right, I had to admit it. That speech, and Billy sounding like he might be crying, got to me. I really did love that man. So I decided to listen to the message again. Tears streamed down my face as I listened, and his message gripped me so much that I didn't even hear the sound of the siren getting closer and closer to me.

CHAPTER THIRTY-FIVE

THERE I SAT, blubbering in my car, tears streaming down with Bingo wiggling in my lap and trying to lick them off, when someone ripped open my car door. Before I even knew what was happening, a big hand reached in and pulled me out of the car and into his arms. Billy. Hugging me and kissing me all over, and Bingo still in the car, barking at the two of us.

"I'm sorry, I'm sorry. Please forgive me. I love you. I love you so much. And I was so worried. Tell me you won't do that again."

The siren was still blaring, and the lights were turning round and round making me dizzy. "Can you turn all that off, please? People will think I was trying to jump in the river or something."

"Oh, sure, right, yeah." He turned around, reached into the car, and turned everything off. The ensuing silence was almost intimidating. "When I got the word from Nick that you had parked your car here," he said, "that's exactly what I was afraid of—that you were going to jump in the river."

"It's only like two feet deep down there. I'm not stupid!"

"Yes, yes, I know that, but I was so worried. I didn't know what to think."

"Billy?"

"Yes, darling. I'm so glad you're safe." His arms were back around me, and he was kissing anywhere he could reach. My face, my hair, my ears, my neck, my shoulders.

"Billy, we need to have a conversation. Seriously. We need to talk about this."

With a serious expression on his face, he nodded his head. "Yes, you're right." He looked at his watch. "Let's go to your house." Opening the passenger door of his car, he said, "Come on, you can ride with me."

I shook my head. "Billy, I can drive my own car home. We're two minutes from my house."

Reluctantly, he closed the door and wrapped his arms around me again. "I don't want to take my eyes off you. I'm afraid you'll disappear again."

If he had been my first husband, Eddie, I would have thought he said that to placate me, but Billy was nothing like Eddie, thankfully. And I could see the hurt in his eyes. It almost made me want to get in the car with him just to make him feel better. Almost. "I'll drive right in front of you. I'll go straight home. Okay?"

I could tell he was having a hard time tearing himself away from me. But he nodded, stepped back, turned toward his car, and as I was about to slip in beside Bingo, Billy rushed back over, threw his arms back around me, hugged me tight, and then returned to his car. Something wet had fallen on my shoulder, and it wasn't raining. And Billy didn't drool. It was a tear.

181

As I drove back to my house, I made sure that no car came between our cars. Billy's show of emotion touched me so much that it was almost better than the third message he had left. He really did love me. He wasn't leaving me for his ex-wife. We were still getting married. A huge relief swept over me. My life was still getting better. Aiden and I didn't *have* to go on that world cruise —not that it would have been a bad thing, mind you, but it wasn't my first choice, which was marrying Billy and staying in Rutledge with him.

I pulled into the driveway, and Billy parked in front of the house. He ran over to me and threw his arms around me again. "I thought I had lost you, and that it was my fault."

There was nothing I wanted more in the world than being with Billy, but I looked at him and said, "And it *would have* been your fault."

He looked down and nodded. "I know."

"Let's go in the house and talk."

With his arm around my shoulders and my arm around his waist, we walked into the house with Bingo following, and headed toward the couch. He let me sit down, and then he sank down on one knee in front of me and took my hand.

"Lorry Lockharte, will you do me the honor of marrying me and spending the rest of your life with me?"

"Billy, I think we've already done this."

"I want to make sure your answer is still yes."

"Of course it is, Billy! Now come up here with me. We need to talk." I didn't mean to be short with him, and I was beyond grateful that everything was working out so well, but I was still a little angry at how everything had come down.

Billy kissed my hand, stood up, then sat down beside me and put his arm tight around me. He looked contrite.

"A week ago, we sat just like this on this very couch, and you said to me, and I quote, 'You kept a big secret from me, and I don't believe in secrets between two people who love each other.' And then you said, 'Let's make an agreement right now—no more secrets.' Remember that?"

Billy nodded, but said nothing.

"And you have an ex-wife! And you never told me! And you kissed her! On the lips!"

"It wasn't a big deal, Lorry. Honest. It didn't mean anything."

"Billy, you do know, don't you, that is *exactly* what men say after they have fooled around on their wives." I lowered my voice to mimic a man's voice and said, "It didn't mean anything, honey, I only love you."

"Lorry, you *know* I would never do that!"

"When I saw you kiss her, I wasn't sure, Billy."

"Oh, criminy, Lorry. She's getting married, and she wanted to invite me to the wedding! You're invited, too."

"I'm not going."

Quietly, he said, "And I invited her to ours."

"You what? You invited your ex-wife to our wedding without even talking to me about it?" I tried to pull away from him, but between him sitting so close to me and the arm of the couch on the other side, there was nowhere to go. So I stuck my lip out in a pout and said, "Then I'm inviting Eddie!" It was a stupid thing to say, but I was angry and it just popped out.

Billy coughed trying to suppress a laugh. "You mean Eddie's ghost?" My first husband, Eddie, was dead. "Come on, Lorry. It's no big deal."

"What's a big deal, Billy, is that you kept a big secret from me—even after our conversation about not keeping secrets from each other."

"I'm sorry. It was wrong of me. I admit it."

"Billy, do you have any other secrets? Because I don't."

Billy didn't speak. He just sat there staring at his one hand that was in his lap.

"Billy? You do! You have another secret that you haven't told me! What? Another wife? You've been to prison? Drunk driving? What is it? Spit it out!"

He nodded. "I have a horse."

"A horse! You mean you're addicted to heroin?" I leaned forward and looked at him. Now *that* was something I had never expected.

CHAPTER THIRTY-SIX

"HEROIN? WHAT? NO! I have a horse! You know. Those animals with four legs and a mane and tail."

I couldn't help myself. Leaning over, I burst into laughter, sat back up, threw my arms around Billy and hugged him. Surprised, he looked at me questioningly.

"You're not upset about the horse?"

"I like horses. And Aiden does, too. He'll be thrilled."

"I was afraid you'd be upset about it—that you might not want to marry someone with a horse."

"If it was a heroin horse, then no, I wouldn't. But since it's a mane and tail horse, I'm delighted!" I started laughing again.

"Does this mean we're okay now?" he asked.

"Yes, we're okay," I said, still laughing. With his one arm around me, he squeezed my shoulder. Then I sat forward on the couch. "Wait! If she's getting married and you didn't spend the night with her last night, where were you?"

Billy leaned forward to match my position. "Oh! Yeah! I got a new lead last night!"

We both leaned back. "Cool," I said. "What is it?"

185

"The bullet that killed the old woman? It is from the exact same kind of gun that was in the exhibit!"

"You mean the one that killed the oldest brother fifty years ago?"

"Yes!"

"Wow, that is a good lead. But where did it take you?"

Billy frowned. "Unfortunately nowhere. Nobody knows what happened to the other gun. Supposedly it was sold at some gun show or on eBay or something."

"That's too bad. It sounded promising."

"Yeah, oh well." Billy squeezed my shoulder and tilted his head so that it touched mine. "Hey, how about if I get off early today, and the three of us spend the afternoon together?"

"Three of us," I said, confused. "Billy, you can't mean you and me and Cheryl," I said in a slight huff.

"No! Definitely no! I meant you and me and Aiden. Have you forgotten about *our* son already?"

"No, not forgotten. But Kasey is picking him up from school, and he's spending the night with Lily." Shrugging, I continued. "Last night I didn't want him around when I was so depressed, and I didn't know how I'd be today, either. So I arranged it this way."

Billy frowned. "Would you mind calling Pamela? I'll pick him up and bring him home. We can play his game or something."

"Sure. I can do that." I really didn't want to, though. Usually, any time spent with Aiden was a great time, but since this was already arranged, and I knew Aiden always loves spending time with Lily, I thought it might help get things back to where they were if Billy and I spent the evening alone.

"Great. If I'm taking more time off, I better get back to work now." He stood up and pulled me along with him. Then he wrapped his arms around me in a tight hug. I was going to ask him to loosen up so I could breathe, but I didn't have enough air to get the words out. So it was a good thing when he finally released me and kissed me on the lips. "Aiden and I will see you soon. Here." He looked at me to verify if I was going to be home. I nodded, and he kissed me again and walked out the front door.

As I stood next to the couch, Bingo jumped up on me. "Bingo, I'll be right back to pet you. I have to call the school now." After calling Pamela and telling her that Billy would pick Aiden up instead of Kasey, I had to track Kasey down. She wasn't at home, so I tried her at work. Breathless, she answered the phone. Figuring that she was too busy to talk, I briefly told her that Billy wanted to pick Aiden up, and she said okay and hung up the phone. Since the *incident* a few months ago, Kasey and I didn't talk much. And surprisingly, I had to admit that I missed her. Maybe after more time went by, we could establish a more adult relationship. I hoped so, anyway.

When I sat back down on the couch, Bingo crawled into my lap, and I petted him. And petted him. And petted him. And all that repetitive movement made me tired, and I fell asleep right there on the couch. Some time later, the phone woke me. It was Billy saying he hadn't picked up Aiden, because Aiden chose to spend the evening with Lily instead of us. Billy was a little perturbed, but it didn't surprise me.

"Well, just come over for dinner. I have an idea for afterwards that we'll both enjoy," I told him. He agreed.

187

CHAPTER THIRTY-SEVEN

WHEN BILLY ARRIVED a little after five, I had the table set. I didn't want to put the leftovers out until after I knew how hungry Billy was. It was a pet peeve of mine when somebody gave me more food than I could comfortably eat, so I tried not to do that myself. We ate in agreeable silence just looking at each other. For me, I felt grateful that we were still together, and he hadn't left me for his ex-wife. And I believed Billy was grateful that we were still together, too. When we finished our portions of spaghetti squash pie, I pulled the chocolate cheesecake pie out of the refrigerator.

"We have to leave some for Aiden, but I think we should have some."

"I'm not going to argue with that logic," said Billy.

We both finished our portions of chocolate cheesecake pie, and then Billy reached out for my hand. "So what did you have in mind for tonight?"

My eyes sparkled at Billy. "My notes! I took notes on everything that the old woman said, but I haven't had a chance to follow up on them. Let's go over to the historical society and analyze what I wrote down!"

Aiden called, and Billy talked to him while I loaded the dishwasher. Then I talked to Aiden. He had apologized to Billy for wanting to go to Lily's instead of coming home with us. That did make Billy feel better. Aiden also said it was okay if we finished the chocolate cheesecake pie because he had two Twinkies at Lily's house. Sometimes I hated what went on over there. But Lily was his best friend, so there wasn't much I could do.

Billy, Bingo, and I drove over to the historical society. We parked in the back and entered the building. Because of the recent aborted break-in, Billy insisted on doing a walk-through before I came any farther than the back door. Bingo stayed with me. In a few minutes, Billy called out, "All clear!" so I walked to the foot of the stairs.

All the lights were on, but still, I wasn't comfortable going upstairs alone without Billy. Go ahead, you can call me chicken, but with everything going on, I didn't feel good going up there alone.

"I just checked up there. It's safe," said Billy.

"Please?"

Bingo bounded ahead, and I followed Billy up. While I retrieved my notebook from the desk, Billy stood under the shelf where Rocky hung out and held out his arms. Rocky jumped into them. After Billy put Rocky down, we returned downstairs, with the sound of Rocky and Bingo chasing each other around the big room.

"Let's sit in Petra's office where there's two chairs," suggested Billy.

"Good idea." I sat behind her desk, and Billy sat in the chair in front of her desk. It was a cramped area, and instead of the chair facing the desk, it faced sideways so it could fit.

"Okay, what do you have?"

"The first note is from when she visited here last year. She said 'You're missing two of the suspects up there! One of them is just in the wrong place! Make sure you fix that!'"

Billy stood up, put his hand out, and helped me up. "Let's go look at the exhibit."

We stood in front of it, hand in hand, and nothing made sense. "I don't get it," I said.

Billy shook his head. "Me, either. Two missing suspects. One would have to be the sister—if you're right. What did she mean about one in the wrong place, though? That doesn't make sense at all." He pointed to the row of suspects: Everett, doctor, dentist, and gardener. "It shouldn't matter if they're out of order."

"No, I don't think she meant that." I looked at the exhibit, squinted my eyes—because sometimes that helps me think better—and said, "You know, this isn't the original exhibit that the old woman saw. Aiden and I changed it after Thanksgiving. I sure wish we could ask the old woman what she meant."

Billy's eyes widened, and he looked at me. "We can do almost as good! We can call Petra to see if she remembers what she originally put up here."

"That's a *good* idea. Let's go call her!"

Billy and I walked back into her office and sat down. I punched in Petra's number and put the phone on speakerphone so Billy could hear, too.

"Hello! Who is this?"

"Is that any way to answer a phone, Petra?" I asked.

"Lorry, what are you doing at work this late—or at all? Are you trying to make up for being missing in action all day?"

190

"Listen, I'm here with Billy, and we have a question for you."

"Well, I'm glad you two got it together. You both were making me miserable. And make it a quick question. Mason drove down tonight, and we were in the middle of a discussion."

"Okay, quick. Remember before Thanksgiving when you put the exhibit together after Aiden was injured? Do you remember how it was different from now? Another person or something?"

"Lorry, honestly, this is stupid. How can I remember that? You and Aiden changed the exhibit so many times."

"Just try, Petra. Come on, it's important."

"Lorry, you—and you, too, Billy—are disturbing me and Mason. Disturbance. From the fourteenth century. Meaning violent interruption of peace or unity. And right now, you're interrupting my peace *and* unity. Goodbye!" And she hung up the phone.

"She seemed a little huffy," said Billy.

I nodded and frowned. "She's got her hands full. Her father has been hitting her mother ever since Thanksgiving. And it's getting worse. Her mom wants to leave, but she has no money and no skills. I offered to let her clean my house."

"Good idea. She can clean mine, too. Mention that to Petra when you talk to her." Billy sat up in the chair. "That was a dead end. Let's move on to your next note."

"Okay. The next note is similar to the first—that we were missing two suspects. But this time she didn't say anything about the wrong place."

"That would make sense if you changed the exhibit and took down a picture or something. Maybe Aiden

191

remembers. You can ask him tomorrow." He nodded. "Next note."

"All right, the last note before she was shot. She said 'When are you going to fix the rogue's gallery down here? You're missing two suspects—a man and a woman! And that gun is not the murder—*You*!' And then the shot rang out, and she was dead."

"That confirms your suspicions that one suspect is the sister. The only other woman around was the mother, and she was disabled and in a nursing home. But her second comment about the gun not being the murder *what*? It has to be the murder weapon. What else could it be? But how would she know that just by looking at it? That doesn't make a lot of sense, either. And when she said 'You!' it must mean she knew her killer."

Nodding, I said, "Okay, so she knew her killer. The next question would have to be motive. Why would anyone want to kill the old woman except that she was such a pain in the neck? She had no insurance or any money to pass on."

Billy cleared his throat. "Ahum, Lorry, I never told you the old woman had no insurance. Did you ask Jacqueline?"

I shrugged and tried to smile my most coquettish smile. "Um, yeah."

Billy shook his head. "So unless she did something to tick someone off enough for them to kill her, it would make sense that her murder was connected to the old murder. And that would be especially true since someone did try to get into the exhibit to steal the gun."

"Yeah, oh, where did you end up putting the gun?"

"Why?"

"Oh, that jerk Howard Strong came in to see the exhibit, and he wondered."

Billy raised his eyebrows and nodded. "Whatever." Billy moved in his seat like he was uncomfortable. There wasn't much room to move. He had squished himself into that small space. He was a big guy, and it was a small chair and small area.

"But what she said about the rogue's gallery. If the motive for the first murder was greed, then it would propel someone from rogue to riches. Maybe even two people were in on it. Rogues to riches."

"Two people? Yeah, that's possible." Billy stood up. "I think we've covered all we can cover. Let's get Bingo, lock up, and go home. It's been a long couple of days."

"I'll say."

CHAPTER THIRTY-EIGHT

WHEN WE GOT back to my house, we sat on the couch and talked about us. Nothing about the murder or what we had or hadn't discovered by going to the historical society. Just us. And it felt good. Billy suggested that maybe later in the week, we would make a trip to Coyote Moon to get a marriage license. We would take Martha and Hugo if they were available. And Aiden. He would want to come, too, for the momentous occasion. And once we had the license, then we could decide where and when we would get married. We would get that one thing out of the way, and it would be one step closer to us being married.

After he left, I lay in bed thinking of the murder. The missing female suspect had to be the sister. But since she was gone, that was meaningless. And I didn't remember ever having her picture up in the exhibit, so she could not be the one in the wrong place. What was that about? Too bad Petra couldn't remember. Maybe I'd bug her again later to see if I could wring it out of her. What was really curious, though, as Billy pointed out, was why the old woman had said it was the wrong murder weapon. How could she know?

Bingo cuddled up next to me and started snoring in my ear. It was almost like purring, so I fell asleep listening to that. But I awoke a few hours later eager to check on Aiden, so I hurried into his room and panicked until I got my bearings and remembered where he was. I pulled out his pillow from underneath the bedspread and hugged it. The pillow smelled like him and made me miss him even more. Then I replaced the pillow and pulled the bedspread back over it, because I didn't want Aiden to know what I'd done. He might feel flattered, but it might bother him, too, so I took no chances. I considered getting to school early in the morning and catching him as Kasey dropped him off, just so I could hug him, but it would probably embarrass him. He was only seven, but peer pressure was still tough.

Back in bed, snuggled up beside Bingo, I still couldn't sleep. All these random thoughts kept going through my mind. Nothing about me and Billy, though. What was done was done. He had explained himself and apologized for the way it had come down. And to think that if I hadn't been late getting back from lunch, none of it would have happened. Well, not totally. He still would have had to admit that he kept the knowledge of his ex-wife from me. But, oh well. None of it mattered anymore. Billy loved me, and we were still getting married.

Something bothered me about the murder, but it was nothing I could pinpoint and say *this isn't right*. But there were too many unanswered questions, and it seemed there was no way to get them answered. I moved from my back to my right side to my left side and still couldn't fall back to sleep. Finally, just before dawn, I fell into a deep sleep only to be awakened by the telephone next to my bed.

It disturbed me so much, and it felt so early, that I was going to answer a grumpy "What!" but then I thought it might be Billy, and I didn't want to add any more angst to that story, so I attempted to answer in my sweet, affable voice instead. It didn't get used often, but I still had it for those occasions that I might need it. I had one of those phones with a speakerphone on it, so I pressed the button instead of trying to pick up the receiver. And after I said "Hello?" in my sweet voice, I was very grateful that I did.

"Mommy!" Aiden cried. "I miss you so much!"

"Oh, Aiden," I said, a tear sliding down my face. "I can't tell you how much I miss you, too, Aiden."

"Mommy, after I talked to Sheriff Billy last night, I really wanted to come home, but I didn't want to bother Aunt Kasey or Uncle John."

"Aiden, you should know you can call here anytime and I would pick you up. Anytime!"

"Yes, I know, but I didn't want to disturb you and Sheriff Billy. I know that you don't get to spend much time alone, and I thought it would be good for you to be together without me tagging along."

"You're so sweet for thinking of us, Aiden, but we *always* love to have you tagging along! Please, next time you want to come home—from anywhere—please just call."

"Okay, Mommy. I will. And I have to go get ready for school now. I love you, Mommy."

"I love you so much, Aiden. Goodbye."

"Mommy! Wait! Would you mind meeting me after school so we can walk to the historical society together?"

"Oh, Aiden"—another tear slid down my face—"of course I wouldn't mind! I would be happy and honored to meet you!"

"Thanks, Mommy! See ya then! I love you! Bye!" And he hung up the phone.

I pressed the speakerphone button again to flick it off and turned to Bingo who was still beside me. With my face buried in his silky fur, I cried and cried and cried. At first, I was crying because of how wonderful it felt to love someone who loved you back just as much. Aiden was such a joy. Since he had come into my life, I had been filled with love. And then I cried because Billy and I were getting married, and Billy, too, loved me as much as I loved him. After that, I continued crying because I had Bingo back in my life, because there was a time when I thought I'd never see him again. By the time I finished crying, Bingo's fur was soaking wet, and I had to get up and find a towel to dry him off. I wouldn't try that stunt again!

CHAPTER THIRTY-NINE

SINCE I WAS already awake, I got dressed and left for work. It was way too early to open, but I parked in the back, walked through to the front and out the front door, locking it behind me. Opening the door to the Rutledge Koffee Korner Kafe, I walked in to see Kasey standing behind the counter.

"Hi, Kasey. Thanks again for taking Aiden the last couple of days."

"No problem," she said smiling. "He and Lily love each other so."

The smile was a good sign. We hadn't been on the best of terms lately. Since I didn't want to get into why I had asked her to take Aiden, I said, "How about a cup of coffee and one of those muffin things with egg and ham on it?"

"Sure, I'll get it right now." She scribbled something on a pad, tore it off, hooked it in the window to the grill, and poured me a large cup of coffee. "Here's the coffee. It will just be a minute for the breakfast sandwich."

Two more people had walked up to the counter, and she helped them. By the time, she had gotten them what they wanted, my breakfast sandwich was ready. Kasey put it in a bag and gave me the receipt. While I was paying for it, more people walked in, which I was grateful for. No time for Kasey to ask embarrassing questions. I hurried out and unlocked the door of the historical society.

Since we weren't open yet, and I didn't want anyone walking over and seeing me sitting in the window stuffing my face full of breakfast sandwich, I locked the door and took my coffee and sandwich upstairs to my desk up there. I turned on the computer to prepare for scanning.

Although I donated my wages back to the historical society, I still felt bad about taking yesterday off. When you have a strong work ethic drummed into you, it doesn't disappear just because circumstances change. So I took a sip of coffee and started scanning documents from the *Children* binder.

I heard the jingling of the door and since I had left it locked, I hoped it was Petra. The footsteps sounded like Petra, so I felt better. She came to the bottom of the stairs and called up, "I hope that's you up there, Lorry!" Bingo stood at the top of the stairs, yipped at her, and then ran down for his usual morning petting.

"Oh, good, it is," she said. "What are you doing here so early?"

"Getting work done to make up for yesterday."

"So you and Billy are okay again?"

"Yes, thanks to you. Thank you for filling him in on a woman's point of view. I appreciate that."

"When you staggered out of my office that day, I knew it wasn't pretty."

"Yes, well, anyway, thanks Petra. Hey, did you know about the horse, too?"

"Billy has a horse? Or do you mean he's on crack?"

"Horse isn't crack, it's heroin," I said. "But no, not drugs. It's a flesh and blood, mane and tail horse. So you didn't know then?"

"No. I knew Cheryl, but I knew nothing about a horse."

"Glad I'm not the only one he keeps things from."

"That makes no sense to me, Lorry, but I'll let it go because I need to study. Glad you're okay. Bye." She walked back down the hall to her desk.

Yeah, I guess it didn't make sense. I was Billy's girlfriend, not Petra. And maybe I still felt a little sensitive about him keeping his divorce from me. But did it really matter? It wasn't like he was trying to hide an affair from me or anything like that. I had forgiven Eddie for a lot worse. No comparison. Time to just let it go. And the cool thing was that he had a horse; and I liked horses. Aiden loved them, too. That could only be a good thing.

I continued scanning documents without a break until Billy called around noon. He wanted to know if I had talked to Petra again about the previous pictures in the exhibit. I told him I would and that I would call if she came up with anything. Then I marched my butt downstairs, Bingo following, and walked over to Petra's office. She was busy with her school work, and her back was to me.

"Hey, Petra," I said to her back.

"Hey," she answered without turning around.

"Any chance you remembered anything about the pictures that you originally put up in the exhibit?"

"Not a thing. Sorry. Bye."

Petra had a unique way of dismissing you. She was serious about her schoolwork, and she wasn't about to let anything interfere. The school only offered the opportunity for the online studies to the best and brightest students. And Petra was one of the best and brightest. So I said thank you and returned upstairs to my scanning.

The afternoon passed slowly, because I looked at my watch every thirty seconds. That's an exaggeration. It was really every forty-five seconds. But time to go get Aiden finally arrived, and none too soon, because I was starting to get a repetitive stress injury from looking at my watch too much.

After I snapped the leash onto Bingo's collar, we walked over to the school. We arrived early, and that was okay. At least I didn't have to look at my watch anymore. Ten minutes later, kids started trickling out the front doors of the school. A few more minutes, and I saw Aiden's smiling face, but it wasn't quite smiling. He stood on the top step looking out at the crowd of people. When he saw me, though, a smile spread across his face, and he jumped up and down waving to me. Then he hopped down the steps and ran at me, dodging people in front of him, and leaped into my arms, almost toppling both of us over.

"I missed you so much, Mommy! Thanks for coming to pick me up! And thanks for bringing Bingo!" He slid out of my arms and wrapped his around Bingo, kissing him on the top of his head. Bingo wagged so hard, he almost fell over. Aiden straightened up and grabbed my hand. "Come on, Mommy! Let's go back to the historical society!"

201

He told me about his day at school, what he and Lily had done for the past two days, and about a new book series he was about to start reading. Then we got to the historical society and Aiden ran to the front to hug Petra. He had missed her, too. Aiden was such a sweetheart.

When he walked back down the hall, I was standing in front of the murder exhibit, still trying to figure it out. So much of what the woman said didn't make sense.

"What are you doing, Mommy?"

"Trying to figure out what the old woman meant when she said one of the suspects was in the wrong place."

"Oh! She was talking about the original exhibit that Petra put up, right? Before you and I changed it?" Without waiting for an answer, he grabbed my hand and began pulling me upstairs. "Come on! We can look in the box!"

Picture me with my hand going over my head, because the simplicity of this totally escaped me. There was a box upstairs with everything we had left out of the exhibit. Of course the missing picture would be there. But after dragging me up the stairs and across the room to the back corner where the door to the storage room was, we found it locked up tight.

CHAPTER FORTY

AIDEN LOOKED AT me, momentarily upset, but then his face brightened. "I'll go get the keys!" He ran away before I had a chance to tell him that my purse was upstairs. I walked back to the upstairs desk where I had stuck the purse, and when Aiden yelled up from the bottom of the stairs that the purse wasn't there, I told him to come on up. When he arrived, I held up the purse and smiled. He held out his hand for the keys, and I dropped them into it. Aiden ran for the door, with me tagging behind. Bingo kept up with him, yipping at his heels.

Aiden had the door open and was rummaging through the box when I arrived. It was a big box, and the top half of his body was completely inside the box. Then his head popped out holding a photograph. "This is all I could find, Mommy. No other pictures in there." He handed me the photo.

It was of the attorney on record, Howard Strong. "Yes, I remember it now. We decided since he never had to defend the brother that we didn't need to have him up there."

"Yeah, he wasn't important to the case."

"Unless he was *the suspect in the wrong place* that the old woman talked about." I held the picture in my hand nodding. "Hey, Aiden, any idea why the old woman would say the gun was the wrong murder weapon? How would she know?"

"I know one thing about the gun," said Aiden. "It had a chip in the pearl handle. I saw it when I picked it up before. And I figured that happened when the guy shot himself and it fell to the floor."

"That makes sense. The chip must have been face up in the exhibit, and she noticed that. It's just too bad—" I was about to mention forensics evidence on the gun, and then I remembered. "Aiden, wasn't there a bullet in there, too?"

Aiden dived back into the box and pulled out a smashed up bullet in a small plastic sandwich bag. "Here it is!" He held it up, and I took it out of his hand.

"Perfect. I don't know if Billy can do anything with this, but we should give it to him."

"Let's go over there now! I want to see Sheriff Billy! I miss him, too! And I know he felt bad because I wanted to spend the evening with Lily last night."

"You already apologized for that, Aiden, though you didn't have to. You may be a kid, but you're a human, and if you'd rather stay with Lily, then you should stay with Lily. You're entitled to do something you want to do instead of bowing to what an adult wants you to do. Except, you know, you need to go to school and not do things that aren't safe."

Aiden listened wide-eyed. "So it was okay that I didn't want to come home, then?"

"Perfectly okay! You're a person, too!"

"I'd still like to take this over to Sheriff Billy."

"Let's call him and see if he's there." I held onto the picture and the bullet, and Aiden put the box away and locked the door.

Billy said he was tied up with something and would send his deputy Nick over to pick up the bullet and take it to Coyote Moon for the forensics analysis. After work, he'd meet us at the house for leftover spaghetti squash pie and chocolate cheesecake pie.

"So he'll see us at the house," I told Aiden. "Come here."

Aiden looked at me questioningly but took a step forward.

"And he said to give you this!" And I gave Aiden a big hug, which left him with a huge grin on his face. "So he's not mad at me?"

"Of course not! And listen, I know you're only seven, but it's important for you to realize that you are the only one in charge of your future. Don't let anyone, a friend, a teacher, or your parents, tell you what you should do with your life. That is strictly up to you." I held him by the shoulders and looked into his eyes. "Understand?" He nodded, and I continued. "If you want to be a street cleaner, it's okay. If you want to be a research scientist, it's okay. But the important thing to remember is that it's up to you!"

"Okay, Mommy."

The reason I came down so hard on Aiden about this was because I heard stories about my great-grandfather insisting that his oldest son become a pharmacist, and all the kid wanted was to become a writer. It created a lot of tension, and I never wanted Aiden to have to go through that. Billy and I had never talked about child rearing, but neither of us had ever done or said anything to Aiden that the other disagreed with. So that was good. Billy's disappointment over not seeing Aiden last night was just his emotion, and I wasn't going to criticize him for that. He loved Aiden and would never do anything to harm him.

It was almost 4:00 when we finished going through the box. So for the next hour, Aiden colored and read, and I did more scanning. We got home just before Billy, ate dinner, gorged on dessert, and watched the first Harry Potter movie, with Aiden sitting between Billy and me. We had seen it at least a dozen times, but it was one of Aiden's favorites, and besides, no one felt like a documentary.

When the movie was over, Aiden was almost asleep, but he perked right up when Billy said we should talk about where we were going to live once we got married. We had talked about it before, but had never come to any conclusions. Billy said that since he expected us to be married soon, we should talk about it with serious intent, whatever that was.

"So where would you like to live, Lorry?" Billy asked.

"In the Lockharte mansion!" Aiden squawked.

Billy and I both laughed. "Aiden, who would clean up the place? We'd have to invite *everyone* we know to share the place, and it would still seem empty!" I said.

"You grew up there," Aiden answered.

"True, but we had servants, and there's no way I want servants. You're *my* little boy. *No one* is going to take the job of raising you away from me."

"What about Sheriff Billy?"

I looked at him and smiled. "We'll share. I'm okay with that. Besides, somebody already lives there."

"No! They've moved out, and it's for sale!" Aiden piped up.

"For sale, huh? I drive by that place every day, and I've never noticed a sign. What makes you think it's for sale?" Billy asked Aiden.

"I heard about it at school. It was private showings only, but since they didn't get many viewers, they just put out a sign."

"Well, even so," I said, "it's out of the question. Not really my kind of place." Billy nodded in agreement.

Aiden shrugged. "It would have been really cool to live there, though."

"Cool isn't the word I would use," I said. And then to Billy, "I love this house. I wouldn't mind staying here."

"And you're sure you don't want to live in my house after I finish it? It's much smaller than the Lockharte mansion, but it's really comfy, and I can change anything to exactly the way you want it." Billy's house was on the same street as the Lockharte mansion, but he had bought it as almost a fixer-upper and had been working on it for months. Since he and I had gotten together, though, it limited his time there, because we spent so much time together. Still, it was getting close. But there was something about it, nothing I could specifically say, but something that made me uncomfortable about it.

I smiled and shook my head. "No, it wouldn't feel like home to me."

"I like it!" said Aiden. "And I can say that I helped fix it up!" Aiden occasionally went over with Billy on weekends and helped him with some of the simpler projects.

"What don't you like about this house?" I asked.

"I need an office, as well. There's just not enough room."

"We can put another desk and computer into my little office."

"*Little* is the problem, Lorry. If there were two desks in there, neither of us could turn around."

My shoulders slumped. I loved my little house. "Yeah, I guess you're right."

"Well, I may have a good alternative that you might just like. Both of you," Billy said.

CHAPTER FORTY-ONE

THE FOLLOWING DAY began with Aiden climbing into bed with me in the morning, which he normally didn't do. Bingo jumped right up on the bed with him.

"I love you, Mommy."

"I love you, too, sweetie."

"I missed you so much. It was only two days, but I missed you!"

"It was a long two days for me, too. I'm glad you're back home now."

"Me, too. Can I have pancakes for breakfast?"

We were cuddling, but I sat up just enough to get both hands around his waist, and I tickled him. "You're just trying to get one over on me, aren't you?"

He giggled and said, "Yes, but I really did miss you!"

"All right, let's get up now. Your choice for breakfast: eggs or cereal."

"Cereal, but I'd rather have pancakes!" He jumped out of bed just in time to miss me giving him a love swat on his behind. Bingo yipped and followed him out of the room.

Aiden and I ate our breakfast—me, eggs; him, cereal —and got dressed and ready for our day. Aiden wore his favorite Rutledge Historical Society sweatshirt, blue jeans, and his Van's tennis shoes, and I wore my favorite dark purple skirt with a light purple sweater, and purple shoes to match.

We drove to the society, parked, and the three of us walked to Aiden's school to drop him off. On the way, we told stupid jokes. Well, Aiden and I did; Bingo just listened—but all three of us laughed at the punch lines! I kissed Aiden goodbye, watched him walk inside, and then walked back smiling. I loved that kid. He made me laugh, he made me think, and he was so easy to love.

I walked in the back door, down the hall, and found that Petra was already at her desk. "Hey, Petra."

"Hey, yourself, Lorry."

"Petra, you've been cranky again, lately. Are you fighting with Mason or is this more family issues?"

"Mason and I don't fight. Nuff said."

"Did you tell your Mom that I'd hire her to clean my house? And I forgot to tell you that Billy said she could clean his, too."

Petra turned around to look at me then. "Things are going better with my dad. He's on his best behavior right now. So she thinks she shouldn't start anything."

"You mean he quit drinking?" That would be surprising news, since Petra's father was the *official* town drunk. Or one of them, anyway.

Petra laughed. "Nothing that drastic. He just stopped beating on her. She can stand him being a drunk, but not the hitting."

"Yeah, I'm sorry to say that I understand that perfectly." Eddie never hit me, but he was a terrible womanizer, and I just put up with it. "Let me know if she changes her mind."

"Sure." She turned back to her computer. "Thanks, Lorry."

It was still a few minutes before opening time, but I unlocked the door and turned the sign to *Open*, anyway. Then I slipped my purse in the bottom drawer, turned on my computer, and waited for it to start up. I was about to click on my email when the door opened, jingling as it went, and Kasey bounded in. She had been standoffish for a while now, but was getting over it.

"Have you heard?" she said, barely able to contain her excitement, "Someone wants to buy—"

The phone rang, and I turned away. The caller wanted our hours and other information about the society. While I was answering the questions, Kasey waved and walked back out the door. After hanging up the phone, I turned to my email. Mason had sent me an article on why it's good to have your children know how to play chess. He and Petra were instrumental in teaching Aiden how to play chess. I didn't want to, but while Aiden was injured, they taught him, and he enjoyed it. But he didn't play often anymore—his choice, not mine. I read the article and answered the email with some smart aleck comment. Then I looked at a forward from Petra of cute animals and cute sayings in speech bubbles above them.

I closed my email just as the door jingled again. Although I thought it was Kasey again to finish her story, instead it was two men. An older man in a black suit with a red tie, and a younger man who resembled him wearing a dark blue suit. It looked like his son.

211

"Good morning! Would you like to see the exhibit area? It's straight back there." I pointed down the hallway.

"No," the older man said. "I want to look at the building."

The younger one shrugged and explained, "He likes to look at old buildings."

They walked down the hallway, and I followed. Not even glancing into the exhibit area, the old gentleman said, "Can we look around upstairs?"

"Sure," I said, "Go ahead." Since I had finished checking my email and was ready to start scanning again, I followed them up the stairs.

I sat at the upstairs computer and turned it on. They walked around, but there wasn't much to see except a bunch of empty shelves, and other shelves full of binders. I heard them try the door to the other room.

They called out, "Hey, can we get in here?"

My purse and keys were downstairs. And since these two weren't the most polite people in the world, I wasn't going to go out of my way to help them see what was a big almost-empty room. "No, I don't have the keys right now."

The older man started to argue, but the younger one said, "Let's just go, Dad," and led the way downstairs. When they got to the bottom, one of them—probably the older one—called up, "Can we get into the private area?"

Before I had a chance to answer, Petra called out from the front, in a voice louder than I had ever heard her before, "No! It's private!"

CHAPTER FORTY-TWO

THE MEN LEFT, and I went back to my scanning until the door downstairs opened again, and I could hear Jacqueline Pennington's voice downstairs asking for me. "Up here, Jacqueline! I'll be right down!" I finished the document I was on and then walked downstairs.

"Good morning!" I said when I saw her. She was dressed in an expensive and stylish navy blue suit.

"Hi, Lorry. I wanted to update you on the will. The reading was yesterday. No clues."

"Nothing at all about the murder and who she suspected?"

Jacqueline smiled. "Oh, yes, there was something about the murder. In the will and I quote 'Jacqueline Pennington is entitled to all my worldly belongings, if, and only if, she continues to pursue the rightful murderer of my father.' The real crazy part is that she has no worldly belongings. Her clothes are it." Jacqueline shook her head sadly. "Poor Mom."

"I'm sorry, Jacqueline," I said.

Jacqueline brightened and looked at me. "Oh! There is something else. A real bright spot in all of this.

Remember that stranger at the reception? You remember, right?" She nodded to me eagerly. "I told you he had attended the memorial service even though it said it was private? Well, you'll never guess who he is."

I shrugged. "I have no idea."

"He's my father! My mother always said he was some no-account drunk who probably died of cirrhosis of the liver. Turns out he's a wealthy manufacturer who lives in New York City. He said that he wanted to marry my mother, but she didn't want to. He didn't even know she had a baby. Mother never told him that she was pregnant. So having a daughter was too much of a shock to say anything at the reception, but he called me today. He's flying in from New York this weekend, and we're going to meet."

"Jacqueline, that's great! I'm so happy for you."

"Lorry, one more thing. I didn't want to bother your boyfriend, but could you give me an update on my mom?"

"Sure!" She was the daughter of the deceased, so it didn't seem wrong to give her an update. "We went over everything your mother said while she was here. It took awhile, but we figured some things out. Aiden found the bullet from the murder fifty years ago, so Billy is having it analyzed for ballistics." I wondered if I should go on. The next thing would be her uncle's—great uncle, really —picture being out of place, which would indicate that he was a viable suspect. It wasn't that I really thought the old codger was a viable suspect, but still, it was *her* uncle.

She heard the hesitation in my voice and said, "Look, I'm not saying anything to anyone. I rarely talk to my uncle. Out of nowhere, he invited Mom and me to dinner the night before she was killed. That and the

214

memorial service were the only times I've seen him in years. He and Mom didn't agree on very many subjects."

All that may be true, but I still didn't think it was wise to tell her that her uncle was a suspect. I didn't think Billy would do that. So instead, I told her something safe. The woman was dead, so what could it matter? "Well, your mother indicated that a woman should be one of the suspects, and that would probably be your aunt, but since she's dead, that's, uh, pardon the pun, a dead end."

"Dead? Aunt Evelyn isn't dead."

That woke me up without the benefit of a cup of coffee. "What do you mean? Howard Strong told me she was gone."

Jacqueline nodded her head. "Oh, yeah, gone. That's what Uncle Howard calls it. She has dementia and is in a nursing home."

"So she's alive?" That got my interest up and my voice rose with my enthusiasm.

"Definitely alive." Jacqueline looked at me. "I could take you to see her, if you want."

Still looking at Jacqueline, I said, "Petra?"

"Yes, Lorry, I'll take care of it. Visitors bother me less than you do!"

Jacqueline raised her eyebrows to me at that, and I said softly so I *thought* that Petra couldn't hear, "She's got issues."

"I heard that, Lorry!" Petra said.

"Well, you do!"

"I know I do, but you don't have to advertise it all around the whole town! Just leave, would you?"

I pulled my purse out of the drawer, opened the door for Jacqueline, and followed her outside. "Do you mind driving or should I?" I asked.

"I'll drive. My car is right here."

She pressed a button on her keys, I heard a beep from a car parked in front of the cafe. It was a sleek metallic silver, and when I opened the door, it had a pristine cream interior.

After I slid into the seat, I looked around. "Wow, what kind of car is this?"

"It's a Tesla Model S electric car. I wanted something that was fancy, but not ostentatious. And it had to be practical for my business. This car holds five adults and two children. Often, clients will drive their own cars, but sometimes it's easier if I just drive them."

"So where are we going?"

"A nursing home in Coyote Moon."

She pulled out onto High Street, turned left on Bridge, and continued east on Broadway. A few minutes later, we were in the heart of Coyote Moon. We chitchatted along the way, her not mentioning the murder, and me avoiding it. I thought we could talk about teachers at the high school, but she had grown up in Coyote Moon. As her mother put it, "I wouldn't live in that miserable, no-good town if you paid me!"

When I told her that before I moved back to Rutledge, I had spent ten years in Coyote Moon, we had some— literally—common ground to talk about. Then, I don't know how it came up, but it did, and I told her about my life with Eddie.

She said, "That's why I've never regretted not getting married."

"I just made a really bad choice. Life with Billy will be nothing like that."

"But how do you know?"

216

"Because Eddie was horrible *before* we got married, and then just got worse! Billy is wonderful now, and I have no reason to believe he won't continue to be wonderful. It's a matter of choices. Just don't make the wrong one!"

Jacqueline turned then, and I was grateful the conversation could move onto something else. "We're almost there," she said.

A few minutes later, we drove under a big entrance sign that said *Welcome to Millennium Village*. She pulled up in front of an immense building with a wide manicured lawn in front of it. That is, you could have called it manicured if it wasn't winter. In January, even in Arizona, lawns were more brown than green. A young man in a red uniform came out and opened my door and then walked around and opened Jacqueline's.

"Hello, Miss Jacqueline," he said.

"Hi, Caleb. Thank you."

Jacqueline joined me on the other side of the car, and Caleb drove the car away. I looked after it in disbelief. "Valet parking?" I asked. "At a nursing home?"

"Uncle Howard only does everything first class. He said there's no reason to lose dignity when you've lost everything else."

"You mean he owns this place?"

She nodded. "He had it built after he had Aunt Evelyn in Coyote Moon Assisted Living and Memory Center. She didn't do well there, and the conditions were horrible. So Uncle Howard made it right."

It made me think that maybe Howard Strong was an all right guy after all. Just because he was a womanizer who came onto sixteen-year-old girls didn't necessarily mean he was an all bad guy. "Wow," was the only response I could think of.

CHAPTER FORTY-THREE

SUDDENLY, I TENSED. He may be an all right guy, but I didn't want him to know I was here asking questions about the murder. "We won't run into him today, will we?"

"Oh, no. He never misses a Tuesday or Friday. Those are his days to visit. When I come see Aunt Evelyn, I always come on Monday, Wednesday, or Thursday. So this is perfect."

I relaxed some but looked around for him, too. The massive wooden doors swung open as we approached them. When I stepped back wide-eyed, Jacqueline just smiled.

"The best of everything. Literally."

Inside the heavy doors, highly polished tile covered the floors. When I thought how stupid that was to make the floors a slippery surface when old people aren't always steady on their feet, I decided to bend down and feel it. Although it might have made me look like an idiot, I wanted to know! It didn't make sense to have the best of everything if the best of everything made walking difficult or dangerous to the people you want to serve.

When I put my fingers on it, I was astonished. It looked highly polished, but not only was it anti-slip, it also had an almost cushiony feel to it.

"Uncle Howard had it specially made." Jacqueline smiled at me.

Standing up, I continued looking around. The textured wallpaper was of a pastoral scene with black and white cows grazing on green pastures. It was very relaxing to look at. To the left of where we stood was a front desk, like in a hotel.

When we started to walk past, the woman looked up and said, "Hello, Jacqueline. Your aunt is doing really well today."

"Thanks, Milicent."

Straight ahead was a large dining area that looked like it was from a five-star restaurant. And right next to that was another large room with a big glass window facing the hall where someone was on stage telling jokes to a wheelchair-bound audience.

"What's down that way to the right?" I asked when we had turned to the left.

"That's the assisted living section. My aunt is in the memory care unit."

"Will she recognize you?"

"Sometimes she does, sometimes she doesn't. Sometimes all in the same day. But Milicent said she's doing well today, so we can only hope."

"What makes it change?"

"Something stresses her out. It can be as simple as someone sitting in her seat at dinner. Who knows?"

We walked through a door with a keypad on the inside, so you could go in, but you had to key in a code to get out. Most of the doors of the residential rooms were closed, but in the ones that were open, I saw large windows letting in light and a landscape painting covering an entire wall.

Turning to Jacqueline, I said, "That is really cool."

"Every resident has a choice of landscapes. They're made of easily removable vinyl, so the residents can change as often as they like." Several nurses passed us in the hall. They all acknowledged us, and several of them spoke to Jacqueline by name. Finally, she stopped in front of a closed door. "Here we are."

Jacqueline opened the door, stepped in, waited until I was in the room, and then closed the door. If she locked it, I didn't know. But it gave me a minute of panic. Maybe I was wrong about Jacqueline's innocence, and this was just a setup so they could kill me and bury me on the grounds. Who would know? Okay, maybe I'm getting carried away. They would probably dump me somewhere the buzzards could pick my bones clean.

Entering the room, the bright light dazzled me, but the picture on the wall stunned me. It was a full wall of ocean, with a big wave rolling in and seagulls gliding through the air. There was a little crab on the beach, and a dolphin under the water that you could barely see. But he was there. It was so real that you could practically hear the crash of the waves and the sound of the seagulls' cries, and feel the sand beneath your feet.

The woman in the wheelchair looking out the window didn't turn around when we came in. Jacqueline walked over to her, leaned down, and kissed her on the cheek. "Hello, Aunt Evelyn," she said quietly.

The woman shook her head like she had been sleeping, which I think she was, and looked up at

Jacqueline. "Oh, Jacqueline! How nice to see you! It's been so long! I've missed you."

Jacqueline knelt down and took Evelyn's hands in both of hers. "I missed you, too, Aunt Evelyn. I'm sorry I haven't been here. You weren't doing so well last time I was here."

Evelyn shook her head. "I know! I'm in and out, aren't I? Half the time I don't know who I am. But regardless, I'm always happy to see *you*."

Jacqueline stood up and moved her arm to beckon me closer. "Aunt Evelyn, I'd like you to meet my friend Lorry Lockharte. Lorry, this is my Aunt Evelyn."

Evelyn looked up at me, smiled, and held out her hand. "Of the Rutledge Lockhartes?" she asked.

I shook her hand gently. "Yes, Evelyn, that's right." The Rutledge Lockhartes were a well-known breed.

"It was sad about all the death in your family, Lorry. Your father, your sister, and then your mother dying so young. So sad. There was almost that much death in my own family." She shivered. "My two brothers. Such a shame." She turned her head around her, like she was suddenly disoriented. "How did I get in this chair, Jacqueline? Wasn't I just taking a nap? I know I felt tired."

Jacqueline looked at me, frowned, and almost imperceptibly shook her head. "No, Auntie, you were resting in the chair when we came in."

"Oh. Okay." She looked out the window and sighed. "You know," she looked up at Jacqueline with tears in her eyes, "I didn't want him to do it, but he said it would be better for us." She shook her head and then turned her wheelchair toward her bed. "Hand me that box of tissue, will you, Lorry?"

I walked over to her night stand on the other side of the bed, picked up the tissues, and brought them to her. "Here ya go, Evelyn."

"Thank you." She blew her nose and slowly moved her head from side to side. "You know, I've never spoken of it before, but I hate that he did that. At first, he said he would just scare them. That's when he had the brake lines cut on my oldest brother's car. He didn't get hurt, so it didn't bother me so much. I mean, if it didn't hurt him, and it helped us, then that should be all right, shouldn't it?" She didn't wait for an answer. "But then the shooting, and then dear Everett taking his own life. I loved little Everett so much. My little brother. That killed me. Something went out of me when Everett died.

"And then everything happened so fast, I didn't have time to even think. With my mother in the institution— that's what they used to call these places back then—and none of them as nice as this one that Howard had built especially for me, dear man, and then Daddy giving up the business so he could bring Mama home and care for her. So Howard took over the business, and there we were." She shook her head and wiped her nose. "But it was so wrong!"

Tears rushed down her face, and using one tissue wasn't enough, so Jacqueline grabbed one and dabbed at her aunt's eyes, while the aunt dabbed at her nose. Then the tears suddenly stopped. The tissue box dropped to the floor. She looked up at Jacqueline and said, "Nurse, help me into bed, please. I'm tired now."

CHAPTER FORTY-FOUR

JACQUELINE HELPED HER aunt into bed and kissed her on the forehead. I watched as she wiped a tear from her own eye.

Evelyn said, "That's all, nurse. Thank you for your help." Then she turned her back on us, and that was that.

The two of us walked out of the room in silence, with Jacqueline closing the door behind us. We walked down the hallway, passing nurses coming in and out of residential rooms. Jacqueline keyed in the passcode at the door, and we stepped into the bright lobby area.

"Goodbye, Jacqueline," Milicent said. "She's doing good today, isn't she?"

Jacqueline, I could tell, was barely keeping it together. "She was. But she slipped backward rapidly." She shook her head. "Goodbye, Milicent."

As we walked by the desk, I heard Milicent say into a speaker, "Car for Jacqueline Pennington." The front doors opened by themselves to let us out, and a minute later, her car pulled up in front. Jacqueline tipped the attendant as he opened the door for her. I slid into the car, and we drove off.

"I'm so sorry, Jacqueline. I didn't mean to set her off like that."

She glanced at me as we drove under the entrance sign. On the way out, it said *Thank you for visiting Millennium Village.* "That's the funny thing, isn't it, Lorry? You didn't set her off—at least not deliberately or even accidentally. She heard your name and on her own segued from the tragedies in your family to the tragedies in hers. While she was talking, I wondered what would have happened had I just introduced you as Lorry."

"Are you sorry you didn't, then?"

"Are you kidding? We found out what my mother suspected all along, although she'd never come right out and say it. I was just crying in there not because Aunt Evelyn and I were so close—we never were. Mother would never allow it. But I cried because another human being who I knew was struggling so much just to live. It's heartbreaking. But what she just told us—" She shook her head and looked at me. "What are you going to do with the information?"

"Tell Billy of course. But in all honesty, what can he do with information from a woman with dementia? Her testimony wouldn't hold up in court, although Billy would never be foolish enough to try to get her there. So the best this information can do is tell Billy where to keep searching." I got the chills and looked behind us. No one was following, but I still couldn't relax. "It's kind of scary, though, isn't it? Howard Strong did all that terrible stuff, made millions, and has been going about his business all these years, like he was innocent or something. How can someone do that?"

"I don't know. But I do feel better that Aunt Evelyn wasn't in on it. Thinking about her killing her own brothers made me sick to my stomach, you know? So I'm grateful for that one little detail. Still——" She shook her head. "The whole thing is sick."

"Sick, maybe, but greed is one of the top motives for murder."

"Oh, no." Her fingers were white on the steering wheel, and her foot inadvertently lifted from the accelerator pedal.

"Did you forget something?"

Jacqueline stepped on the accelerator again and shook her head. "It just occurred to me. Howard must have killed Mother, too. He knew she was interested in the exhibit and probably thought she might discover something that would reveal him as the murderer." Tears slid down her face. "I can't believe it. He killed my mother."

I reached out and patted her arm, and then we were both silent for a few minutes, letting everything we had just learned sink in. Then Jacqueline looked at me and asked, "Do you mind if I stop and get my dry cleaning on the way back? It will only take a minute or two. It's a drive-thru." Her tears had dried and left tracks on her face, but I wasn't going to say anything.

"Sure. No problem." I looked at my watch, and it was 10:30.

Jacqueline turned right off the main drag toward the dry cleaners. The car phone rang, and she pressed something on the steering wheel to answer it. "This is Jacqueline."

"Hey, Jacqueline, this is Cathy."

"Oh, hi."

"Are you available for a showing?"

"Sure, I just finished with something here in Coyote Moon. Where is it? I'm heading into Rutledge now."

"That's perfect, then. The showing is in Rutledge."

"Oh! It is? Where?"

"It's the Lockharte Mansion over on Hillside Terrace. Do you need the address?"

Jacqueline glanced over at me and smiled. "No, I can find it. What time did they want to meet?"

"Eleven-fifteen."

"That's cutting it close, but I should be able to do that. I just have to make a quick stop at the dry cleaners."

"Do you want me to make it later?"

"No, it's all right. Tell them I'll be there at eleven-fifteen. What are their names?

"Mr. and Mrs. Edwards."

"Okay, thanks, Cathy. Bye!"

She pressed the button on the steering wheel to disconnect the call and glanced over at me. "You heard it, Lorry. I have an appointment at eleven-fifteen to show the Lockharte mansion!"

"Oh, that's so funny! Aiden just told me last night that it was for sale. He wanted to move in there!"

"Really? That's cute." She pulled into the drive-thru lane at the dry cleaners, but there was a big sign in the window: *Closed. Sorry for the inconvenience.* "Oh, shoot! I'll have to go inside now." Driving her car around to the front, she parked in one of the spaces in front of the dry cleaners. "I'll be right back." She pulled a receipt from the bottle holder on the console and jumped out of the car, hurrying toward the door of the dry cleaners.

As I sat in the car waiting for Jacqueline, I went over everything we had learned from Evelyn. I shook my

227

head. Anyone that cold blooded was capable of anything. I'd have to warn Billy about that, but Billy was always careful. The thought of Howard Strong planning and carrying out the murders made me shiver, and I looked around suspiciously, but saw nothing out of the ordinary.

Then I reached into my purse, pulled out my cell phone, and called Billy. Usually, I called his cell phone first, but he rarely answers it when he's working, so I called directly to the sheriff's station. And the line was busy. After waiting a minute, I called again, and it was busy again. That was strange, because they have four or five lines. When I called again, and it was still busy, I tried Billy on his cell.

Finally, he answered. "Hi, babe, gotta run. Something's going on in town. I don't have a minute to talk."

"This will take less than a minute, Billy, and it's important!"

"Sorry, babe, I'm outa here," and he must have handed his phone to the dispatcher, because a second later, she said, "Sorry, Lorry, he just ran out the door. Some car hit a fire hydrant by the high school, and everything is a mess. I'm sure he'll call you back when he's finished there. The phones have been wonky for a while, and now this. Gotta go. Bye!"

I slipped the phone back into my purse and checked my watch. It was already ten-forty, and there was no sign of Jacqueline yet. She would still have no trouble making her eleven-fifteen showing, even with the heavier late morning traffic. Unless, that is, the broken fire hydrant caused any traffic issues.

Jacqueline came running out to the car ten minutes later. "Sorry," she said. "They were really backed up in there because of the broken drive-thru." She opened the back door and hung the clothes on the hook, then slid in the front beside me. After starting the engine and pulling out into traffic, she glanced at me. "Hey, while I was waiting in line, I got to thinking. How'd you like to come to the showing with me? It would be fun for you to see the house again. How long has it been?"

"More than ten years. Mom sold it and moved to the Midwest after I started college in Coyote Moon."

"What do you think? Come on! It will be fun!" She looked at me again and shrugged. "It might even help you get over what we just learned. I know that *I* don't want to think about it."

"Yeah, I tried to call Billy to tell him, but he was busy with some emergency in town. I hope it doesn't make you late for your appointment." I told her about the fire hydrant, and she thought exactly what I thought: if they closed the bridge, she'd be late.

"Will you go? Please? I think you'll enjoy it."

The thought of going to the old *homestead* gave me some kind of a thrill. What kind, I still wasn't sure. It might be fun to look around and see what, if anything, had changed. I did have some good times in that house. They weren't *all* bad times—just most of them. "Yeah, all right. It could be interesting, and Aiden will love hearing about it."

It was after eleven when we reached the backed up traffic leading across the bridge, which was closed, as we had feared. There weren't many cars waiting, though, so it hadn't been closed for long. The Lockharte mansion was less than five minutes from the bridge, but there was no telling how soon it would open. Jacqueline kept looking at her watch, even though there was a digital clock on her dashboard. Traffic still wasn't moving, and the clock said it was already eleven-ten.

"Oh, I hate being late to a showing."

"It's your own business, right? So you won't get in trouble from anyone if you're late?"

She chuckled. "No, I won't get in trouble. But prospective buyers are sometimes funny about that. If they expect you at eleven-fifteen and you don't show up until eleven-twenty or eleven-thirty, they might leave or if they stay, they might walk through the house and look for reasons not to like it. I'm not late often—usually a situation like this that is out of my control—but I have lost sales before. And selling the Lockharte mansion would be a huge commission for me. I'd hate to lose it."

It was eleven-twenty when traffic started moving across the bridge, but it was one car at a time and unbearably slow. Jacqueline was about to have a conniption fit—whatever that is—by the time we drove across the bridge and turned left onto Hillside Terrace.

CHAPTER FORTY-FIVE

THE GATES STOOD wide open, and Jacqueline pulled into the wide circular driveway. It surrounded a center area made up of xeriscaping and a large unique fountain featuring a dragon with golden wings outstretched, and instead of fire coming out of his mouth, a stream of water shot out and mixed with the water in the bottom of the pool. When my father was alive, he would sometimes have coloring put in the water, and that made the dragon look especially cool.

What caught my attention as we drove in was the color of the house. "They painted it purple!" I exclaimed. It was a beautiful shade of lavender with dark purple around the windows.

"Oh, no!" said Jacqueline. "I can't believe anyone would make an offer on the house looking like this."

"I like it!" The color made me smile. "And it matches my outfit!"

Jacqueline laughed at that and looked at me all dressed in purple. "The prospective buyers must have gotten caught up in the traffic jam, too, thankfully. I'm so glad I'm not late. But instead of waiting for them outside, let's go in so I can look around. Usually, I check out a house before I show it, but today I had no time for that."

I got out of the car, still aghast at being here in front of the Lockharte mansion where I had grown up. It was a huge Victorian, three stories, with a circular tower in the center front that rose above the third story. The tower had a metal cap on the top that resembled a royal crown. It was painted dark purple to match the window trim. There was even a left wing and right wing to the house. Now that I saw it in what I felt was an objective manner, it really did look decadent. Although I couldn't see them from where I stood, I knew there were servant's quarters in the rear. And when we lived here, those quarters were always full—even after my father and sister died, and it was just my mom and me in the house. She always said that we had to look respectable. She and I were so different.

Jacqueline walked up onto the front porch replete with rockers and a porch swing, advanced to the door, and rang the bell. "It's supposed to be empty, but I like to be sure before I use the key." No one answered, and she used the lockbox that was under the farthest rocker. A padlock secured it to the heavy metal rocker.

She turned around to look at me. "You ready?"

I smiled and had to suppress an urge to giggle. "Yeah, let's go." Sometimes giggling is not appropriate.

She stuck the key in the lock, turned it, pressed the lever on the big brass door handle, and it swung open showing the open expanse within. We walked in and Jacqueline said, "Wow. Nice."

She wasn't looking at the floor, but I was. It was white and black marble in two foot squares. My father used to

232

say it reminded him of Alice in Wonderland. He liked Alice in Wonderland. He said the problem with adults was that they lost their sense of wonder, and him putting in this black and white checkerboard floor was a reminder never to do that.

Jacqueline was looking at the two staircases leading upstairs. My father used to say, one for going up and one for going down. They were on either side of the room surrounding a large center area. The stairs were white, the railing was black wrought iron with intricate patterns, and it extended in both directions at the top of the stairs, making a balcony and passage to the left wing and the right wing. On either side of the staircases were open doorways leading to the rest of the house.

In the center area, between the two staircases, was an elegant round table that we never used. My father had images of playing poker there, but aside from once when we first moved in, that never happened, either. Above the table, hung a humongous chandelier with crystals hanging down in patterns that made it look like a waterfall. It was magnificent. It—besides the dragon out front which I loved—was one of my favorite things about the house. When you sat on one of the easy chairs at the edges of the room and looked up, you could almost hear the thundering of the water coming down.

The silence in the house was disconcerting. Some would call it peaceful, but when you grew up here and were used to the hustle and bustle of people all the time, it just didn't feel right. There were always servants and service people wandering through the great halls of the house, because my mother had a penchant for remodeling. That didn't start until after my father died— he liked it the way he had built. But I always thought she did the whole remodeling pursuit just to have something to do.

Jacqueline and I stood there, neither of us moving or talking, just absorbing the feel of the place. And then I heard it. Softer at first and then louder as the footsteps got closer. Jacqueline said, "I wonder who that could be. No one should be in here right now."

CHAPTER FORTY-SIX

JACQUELINE MAY NOT have known who it was, but I did. I recognized the tap tap tap, and it wasn't the raven. It was *his* patent leather shoes.

Howard Strong, dressed in painter's overalls, came walking out from the left doorway holding the pearl-handled revolver which, I was sure, was the murder weapon of Edward Pennington *and* Virginia Pennington. I could see his red power tie beneath the overalls that had light and dark purple paint on them. So he must have found them at the premises and slipped them on— probably to avoid blood spatter on his clothes.

For a quick instant, I remembered how Jacqueline had convinced me to come to this showing, and I thought maybe the two of them had set me up. But when I looked over at her, she looked even more afraid than I felt. If only I had had the chance to tell Billy, then he'd come out of nowhere and save us. Instead, he was probably officiating traffic at a broken fire hydrant.

"Uncle Howard," Jacqueline began, her voice quivering, "who will believe an old woman with dementia?"

Stupidly, I turned to Jacqueline. "I thought you said he didn't go there on Thursdays? How would he know we were even there?"

Howard smirked. "I just happened to have a meeting tomorrow, so I decided at the last minute to visit my dear wife today. How convenient that was."

"I already told Billy about our conversation with your wife. He'll be here any minute."

Howard laughed. "How stupid do you think I am, Lorry? You don't make as much money in business as I did, and plan and carry out two murders without getting caught, without being pretty darn bright." He pointed to his head with the gun. "I have a higher IQ than God." As he pointed the gun back at us, he looked at me. "Lorry, why did your eyes just get so big?"

"I was hoping the gun would go off when you pointed it at your head."

"No such luck. I always make sure to arrange everything to perfection. I leave nothing to chance." He shrugged. "That's how you get away with *murder*." He looked at Jacqueline. "You know in real estate, it's location location location? Well, with murder, it's plan plan plan. Or control control control. And I plan and control every detail.

"Take for instance, today. When I saw you both there —at Millennium—I immediately called my contacts at the phone company to block the lines of the sheriff's station. And I instructed Leonard to take one of my cars and *accidentally* have an accident just inside Rutledge town lines—where the consequences might be closing the bridge. Timing had to be perfect, of course. I had to be on this side of the bridge before that happened. But by the time Leonard ran into that fire hydrant, I was already safely in place." He laughed.

"Making the appointment to see this house? Sheer genius, even if I do have to say so myself. And Mr. and Mrs. Edwards? I thought that was a nice touch, since Edward was the first one that I killed." Then he looked at me. "I knew you grew up here and would want to see it again. It was perfect! Killing two birds with one stone, so to speak." Howard waggled the gun at us. "Right, birdies?"

He laughed again. I would like to say it sounded like an evil, demented laugh, but it only sounded like the laugh of a normal eighty-year-old man. Not that Howard Strong was normal, you understand.

"If you're so smart and all, how could you possibly know Jacqueline would be sick so you could kill her mother at the society?"

Jacqueline shook her head. "I can tell you that, Lorry, although I didn't figure it out until this minute. Remember I told you that Howard had invited us to dinner the night before? He gave me chocolate candy— my mother was never a fan of candy, and Uncle Howard knew how much I loved it, because he used to give it to me when I was a kid." She pointed to Howard and continued, "That was Ex-Lax, wasn't it? Very clever, Howard. I ate so much, I could have died. That would have ruined your plan right there, because I couldn't have taken Mother to the cafe."

"No, no, no, dear Jacqueline. Everything was perfect. I only put out enough *candy*, hey hey, to get you good and sick, but not sick enough to deny that crazy old woman. I knew how intent she was on seeing the exhibit."

"You're sick, Uncle Howard."

I found it interesting how she kept calling him Uncle Howard even while he was pointing a gun at her. And for his part, he called her "dear Jacqueline" like he really liked her.

As if he had read my mind, he said, "Oh, dear, dear Jacqueline. I always liked you, you know that? You were such a cute kid. Too bad *she* was your mother. You might have turned out all right.

"But you have to understand that wanting money, power, and influence is not a sickness. It's a goal. And it has been my goal ever since I can remember. Your Aunt Evelyn was part of that goal. But I loved her very much. She learned to appreciate what I had done and what it allowed us to become in this world. Evelyn always supported me, as I knew she would. She's that kind of woman.

"Nothing like your mother!" He glared at Jacqueline. "She was so intent on proving that her father was innocent. Do you know how young she started on that crazy crusade? I don't think she was even a teenager yet when she decided that I was the killer." He looked at Jacqueline and tilted his head in confusion. "She never told you who she suspected, Jacqueline?"

"Never. I knew she didn't like you, but she never told me why."

"Well, now you know why. A lot of good it will do you though. Imagine, her accusing *me* of the murder. Sweet, innocent, lovable, upright, me. It was laughable, honestly. *I* was the one who always defended Everett when anyone spoke against him. *I* was the one who was supposed to defend him in court. And it was Everett, himself, who ruined that one for me."

238

Howard closed his eyes and turned his head back and forth. "I had such a brilliant strategy planned for court. It would look like I had everything but an airtight alibi for Everett. Everyone would be assured of my victory. And then, at the last minute a credible witness would step forward to say that he had seen Everett leaving the house at the time of the murder." He winked at us. "It's amazing what a little money can get people to say. It would have been the best—and most profitable—case I ever lost. And that coward Everett had to ruin everything by killing himself. It was a shame. But it amounted to the same thing though. I got what I wanted. The family fortune.

"Well, ladies, I wasn't going to kill you, but now that I've told you all my secrets, I have to!" He chuckled to himself like he was the cleverest thing. Then he waved the gun in the air. "Come on, the official deed will be done in the servants' quarters." He pointed to the floor and shrugged. "I wouldn't want to stain this beautiful marble floor. I do have some sense of decency."

"Honor among murderers, huh?" I said.

I really didn't expect Billy to come and rescue me, but when he did, it didn't amaze me, either. That was Billy: he was always there when I needed him.

I heard him say, "Now!" And he and Nick appeared in opposite doorways with their guns drawn and pointed at Howard. "Put the gun gently on the ground, Mr. Strong. I don't want to hurt the marble, either, but I won't hesitate to shoot you center mass and clean up afterward."

Howard's little revolver looked pitiful next to Billy's big Glock, and no one was surprised when he laid it gently on the floor and raised his hands over his head.

239

Nick kicked the gun toward Billy, grabbed Howard's arms, put them behind his back, and snapped cuffs on them.

"I don't understand, Sheriff," Howard said to Billy. "How could you possibly have known I was here? I didn't even know myself until a little while ago."

Billy picked up the gun and walked toward me, his gun still aimed at Howard. "I've had you followed for days, Mr. Strong. You were at Millennium Village at the same time as my prospective bride. She has a nasty habit of being on the wrong end of a pointed gun. And when I found out that it was your son who caused the accident at the high school, the rest wasn't too difficult to figure out."

Howard shook his head. "I don't understand. My plans always worked perfectly before."

"*Before* being the salient word," I said as Billy holstered his gun and wrapped his arms around me.

CHAPTER FORTY-SEVEN

JACQUELINE STOOD NEXT to us softly weeping, so Billy put one arm around her, and Jacqueline and I put an arm around each other, and we stood there in a three-way hug.

"I thought that was it," said Jacqueline. "And I thought he was going to kill us—just like he killed my mom and my grandfather." She burst out in sobs, and Billy and I both squeezed her to us.

"I wasn't going to let that happen, Jacqueline," said Billy.

"I can't believe he was even here waiting for us!" I said.

"The problem, my dear bride, is that you underestimated him, just like he underestimated me." Billy kissed me on the forehead. "That's a dangerous thing to do."

"Apparently." I was the first one to pull away. When Howard had the gun pointed toward us, I didn't realize how fast my heart was beating. But now that I was safe again, I could feel it slowing down to normal.

"Hey, Billy," said Nick. "What do you want me to do with this guy?"

Billy turned around and there stood Howard, hands behind him, head hung low, and Nick's hand holding fast to his upper arm. "I'll go get the car and bring it around. You stay here with him." He turned to Jacqueline and me to escort us out the front door. "And you two, get along on your way now. Nothing to see here. Lorry, I'll be at the society soon. Get Eddie's death certificate and be ready to go."

"We're going to get the marriage license today?" I asked.

"I'm not waiting another minute. Be ready! I'll arrange everything else."

We got into Jacqueline's car as Billy ran out the front gate. He had probably parked a car somewhere out front before Howard even got to the house, and Howard wouldn't have even noticed another random car on the street.

A white Buick whizzed past us when we drove out through the gate. I didn't recognize the car, so it must have been Nick's. It stopped in front of the door, Billy jumped out, and ran into the house. Jacqueline drove away before I could see the two men bring Howard Strong out to the car.

We didn't say anything on the way to the society, but as she pulled up in front, she said, "We've been through a lot together, Lorry. How about some time after we unwind from all of this, we go out to lunch?"

"I would love to, Jacqueline." Leaning over, I gave her a hug before getting out of the car.

I walked to the door of the society, put my hand on the knob, and turned around to watch Jacqueline drive away. She waved to me through her open window, and I waved back. Taking a deep breath, I stepped through the door and fell into my chair. It had been a powerful morning.

"Hi, Petra," I managed to say. Now that everything was settled and I was safe, I felt like I was falling apart.

"You sound exhausted," said Petra. "You took the whole frickin' morning off!" Before I had a chance to answer, she added, "Exhausted. Mid seventeenth century. Consumed. Used up. So how can you feel exhausted?"

"Petra, you wouldn't believe what just happened."

"Not interested, Lorry. I've got work to do. Somebody has to do it."

I felt too tired to argue or defend myself. She'd find out eventually, and that was fine. I didn't have to prove anything, and there was nothing glamorous in having a gun pointed at you. Unfortunately, I knew that all too well.

As I sat there still feeling like I could barely breathe and that my heart would never stop its rapid thump thump thump in my chest, I saw Billy pull into the space at the front of the society. Hugo was in the front seat, and I watched as Aiden jumped out of the back seat and came running toward the door. He came through it in a rush, practically sending the tinkling bell flying, and then Aiden flew right into my arms.

"Mommy! Mommy! Are you okay? Are you hurt? You almost got killed! Again!"

"What?" said Petra from the other room.

"I'm perfectly okay," I said to Aiden, trying to believe it myself. "Billy had me covered the whole time. You know how he takes care of me."

"*What* is Aiden talking about?" Petra stood by the partition that separated my office from hers. "Aiden? What?"

"My mommy almost got killed *again*! The guy who killed the man in the murder exhibit *and* that old woman was going to kill her because she found out that he did it!"

"Lorry?" Petra looked at me.

Aiden was still in my arms, but I looked above his head and nodded at Petra. "It's all true."

Petra took two giant leaps over to me and Aiden, and threw her arms around us both. Usually we're close, but she still has her moods. Teenagers. Whatcha gonna do?

"I'm so sorry, Lorry. I thought you were just being melodramatic again! I'm so glad you're okay!"

"I'm not melodramatic! I can't help it if people keep trying to kill me!"

Before Petra could give me a smart aleck answer to that, Billy honked his horn. "Oh!" said Aiden. "Sheriff Billy sent me in here to bring you out and remind you to bring Eddie's certificate!"

"I don't know where that thing is!" I said.

"If you're talking about when he died, you put it in your drawer. I think your exact words were 'What do I need this for?'" Petra stood up straight and returned to her office, where she said, "I suppose you're leaving for the rest of the day now."

"Oh!" said Aiden again. "And I was supposed to tell Petra that it's okay to close up if she wants to."

Digging through my top drawer, I found Eddie's death certificate in the envelope it arrived in. Petra was right. I had said that. And now look at what's happening. Just

244

goes to show you that no one knows what the future holds.

Aiden was holding the door open and jumping up and down. "Come on, Mom! Sheriff Billy said to hurry!"

Grabbing my purse and the death certificate, I followed Aiden outside, but not before turning the door sign to *Closed*. I knew Petra wouldn't do it, so I did it for her. I wasn't sure if she liked being a martyr or if she was dedicated. It was probably a little of both.

The doors opened when we reached the truck, and Aiden climbed into the back seat, and I climbed into the front that Hugo had vacated. Billy leaned over and kissed me.

"You brought the certificate?" he asked.

"Luckily, Petra remembered where I put it."

Martha leaned forward from the back seat and squeezed my shoulder. "You okay, Lorry? We heard it was a little hairy over there at your old house."

"I'm not sure if I'd describe it as hairy, but I'm glad it's over and that Billy came in time to rescue us."

"The crime was no fun, a man with a gun," began Hugo in his usual singing jokes, "it may not have been hairy, but it certainly was scary!"

Martha clapped, and I said, "You captured it exactly, Hugo!"

"Sheriff Billy? Can I call you Sheriff Daddy again today since you're going to get your marriage license?"

His little voice was hesitant, like he was afraid to ask. Aiden was as happy that I was marrying Billy as I was. We, Aiden and I, were both getting a really good man, and we both knew it. I just hoped the wedding was soon, because all this rigamarole of waiting around and planning was getting to be a drag. If it was up to me, I'd say let's just do it.

"No, I'm sorry, Aiden, not today." Billy and I both heard Aiden sigh with disappointment. "But don't worry, you won't have long to wait.

"Where are we going, anyway?" Martha tapped me on the shoulder and said, "Billy got me out of a meeting and didn't even tell me why!"

"I'm sorry, Martha! I didn't realize—" Billy said.

"That's okay. It wasn't a very good meeting, anyway. I didn't want to stay." Her voice sounded sad. Or bored. One of the two.

"Well, we're going to the Coyote Moon courthouse to get a marriage license. I wanted to hurry up the whole process before, but now that Lorry almost got herself killed *again*, let's just do it. Then we can go out to lunch. How's that sound?"

"Food always sounds good to me!" said Hugo.

"And I found a place close to the courthouse that serves breakfast all day to satisfy your keto diet, Hugo!" Billy told him.

"Excellent!" said Hugo.

"Then we can talk about where we can have the wedding," said Martha. "I've been thinking about it and have some new ideas."

"I think you're in trouble now, Billy," said Hugo. "Martha's been thinking about it!" Martha elbowed him in the ribs, sending Hugo into a fit of laughter, which made all of us laugh, too. They had a great relationship, and I hoped that Billy and I could have our good relationship last as long as theirs.

"What happened after Jacqueline and I left? And whose car was that?"

"Nick's car. Nick drove back to the sheriff's station with me and Howard Strong sitting in the back seat. Then we switched cars, put him in the back of the sheriff's car alone, and Nick drove him to Coyote Moon. Then I picked up Hugo, Martha, and Aiden."

"What did that jerk say on the way to the sheriff's station?"

"It was like he was broken or something. He kept repeating 'My plans always worked before.'"

"Sick puppy," said Hugo.

We chitchatted the rest of the way to the courthouse, and then Billy parked in the lot. It was the same courthouse I had been to before, but we went to the office area. There was no line for marriage licenses, so we walked right up. Hugo, Martha, and Aiden sat on seats against the opposite wall to wait for us. Before we stepped up to the window, Billy said, "Get your identification and the death certificate ready."

Digging through my purse, I pulled both items out. "All right."

At the window, after the tired looking clerk asked if he could help us, Billy said, "We'd like to get a marriage license, please."

"Seventy-eight dollars, and I'll need to see photo identification for both of you."

Billy handed him the cash and our documents. The clerk counted the money, wrote information down, pushed a button on the computer, waited for the license to print out, and then he handed it to us. I started to walk away, but Billy stayed at the window.

"Is your Justice of the Peace available?"

"You don't have an appointment, do you?" the clerk asked.

"No, but someone told me if he wasn't available, someone else could do it."

"Yes, he's on vacation this week, but there is *someone*."

Billy even asking about this surprised me. He had never mentioned that he wanted to get married today, and Billy was not an impulsive guy. It didn't bother me though. However, the way the clerk said *someone* disturbed me. Who was it, I wondered. An Elvis impersonator or something?

Martha, Hugo, and Aiden were all looking at me, but I shrugged. Then I heard Billy say, "Well, if the *someone* isn't too busy, let's do it right now."

"Let me go talk to Madge," said the clerk. "I'll be right back."

Madge, I thought. So it wasn't an Elvis impersonator. I wasn't sure if I felt relieved or disappointed, but I think I leaned toward relieved.

Billy looked at me and then at Martha, Hugo, and Aiden. "You all ready for this?"

Hugo stood up. "If you mean ready for lunch, yes! I'm ready!"

Billy had a sly smile on his face. "No, I mean to get married." He looked at me and put out his hand. "Come on, sweetie. Let's do this." The way Billy had been pushing to get the license today, this didn't surprise me.

When I put my hand in his, he pulled me to him and kissed me. Then the clerk came back and opened the office door for us.

Before we started down the long hallway, Hugo came up and took my hand out of Billy's. "You can't have her yet, my man. I have to walk her down the aisle—er, hallway." Martha stepped up with Billy, Hugo put his arm through mine, and down the hallway we marched, with Hugo humming *that special bridal song* as we went, and Aiden following behind looking important.

When we entered the conference room where the clerk indicated, Hugo gave me over to Billy, who waited just inside the door. The five of us approached the woman who would perform the ceremony. She was a middle-aged woman, dressed in wrinkled slacks, a half-tucked-in blouse, and a face as wrinkled as her slacks. My first guess was that she was a smoker, and when I got close enough, I found that I was right. Her clothes reeked of smoke. She may not be an Elvis impersonator, but this would be a wedding to remember!

"Hello, I'm Madge," she said. "Which ceremony would you like to have? They cost the same." She handed Billy a brochure, and Billy showed it to me.

"I'm okay with this one," said Billy. He pointed to one that was basically do you, yes, you're married.

I looked at him and shook my head. "That would be my choice, as well," I said.

He handed it to Madge, and she put it down and faced us. We turned to each other, and Billy took my hands. Then he said, "Wait!" He turned to Aiden. "Give it to me," and he put out his hand, palm up. Aiden reached into his pocket and pulled out a ring case.

"You knew," I said to Aiden.

"I didn't know what it was," said Aiden.

"I told him to hold it for me," said Billy. "But I didn't tell him what it was." He took my hands again. "Come on."

The woman said the words with Hugo, Martha, and Aiden looking on. Billy pulled out the ring case at the proper time and took one of the rings out of it. "I didn't think you'd want anything fancy, but I can change it if you want." He showed me a single gold band with a row of tiny white diamonds all the way around—an eternity ring. His ring was exactly the same.

"It's perfect," I said.

Billy slipped it on my finger, I slipped his on his finger, the words were said, the deed was done, and we kissed, sealing the deal. Billy hugged Madge and thanked her, gave Hugo and Aiden a high five, and kissed me again. I got my "I now pronounce you husband and wife," and a great guy to boot. Color me happy—no: ecstatic.

Aiden stepped up to us and looked at Billy. "*Now* can I call you Sheriff Daddy?"

"No, Aiden, you can't. That's not appropriate." Aiden looked so distraught, I thought he might burst out into tears, until Billy added, "Now you can call me Daddy!" And he bent down, scooped Aiden up, and swung him around.

Everybody hugged, and we were about to make our way to lunch, when Martha's cell phone rang. She dug into her purse, pulled it out, held it up to her ear, and said "Hello." Then she nodded her head, said, "Okay, thanks," and hung it up. Now she looked as though she might burst out into tears.

"Martha, what is it?" I asked.

She looked at the floor and shook her head. "The town council has just voted to sell the Rutledge Historical Society."

If you liked this book and feel so inclined, please leave a review on Amazon. Thank you! I appreciate it!

And if you'd like to know when the next Rutledge Historical Society mystery comes out, sign up for the mailing list: http://www.ralstonstorepublishing.com/mysteryL.html

Read the next book in the series: *Secrets for Sale*
The sale of the Rutledge Historical Society has been suspended because the buyer was murdered during the town council meeting. Luckily, after Lorry's emotional outburst, she was talking to the mayor at the time the shot was heard, so she is in the clear. Although all members of the council are under suspicion, everyone suspects someone near and dear to Lorry, forcing her nose, once again, somewhere it doesn't belong.

Jerri Kay Lincoln

Other books published by Ralston Store Publishing:

Time Travel Sweet Romance
Cowgirls in Time Series by Erica Einhorn
A Chill Wind
Wind Beneath My Wings
Against the Wind
The Healing Wind
Ride Like the Wind
Wind of Change
The Way the Wind Blows

Caregiving
The Journey that Matters by Jodie Lightener

Suspense
Darkness in the Light by J.K. Lincoln

India
Not My Guru by Parvati Hill

Women's Fiction/Reincarnation
Two Lifetimes, One Love by Thea Thaxton

Yoga Books
Bathroom Yoga
Airplane Yoga
Wheelchair Yoga
Essential Yoga on Horseback
Exercises for Therapeutic Riding

Spaghetti Squash Pie

1 whole spaghetti squash
1 pound hamburger
2 cups shredded cheese *(you can use 8 ounces cream
cheese if you freeze it for thirty to forty-five minutes
before shredding)
bell pepper cut in small pieces
sliced ripe olives
¾ cup tomato sauce

Easy way to cut spaghetti squash:
1. Preheat oven to 425 degrees.
2. Line a baking sheet with parchment paper.
3. Place the whole spaghetti squash on the baking sheet
and bake for 15 minutes or until soft enough to cut.
4. Use a hot pad or oven mitt to secure the squash while
you carefully slice it in half lengthwise.
5. Scoop out the seeds with a large spoon and save them
for roasting. They're delicious!
6 .Drizzle the squash with olive oil and lightly season
with salt and pepper.
7. Place flesh side down and continue roasting for 10 to
30 minutes, depending on the size of the squash. To
check for doneness, flip one half of the squash over and
run a fork down the side of the squash. If it comes away
from the side easily in a nice spaghetti texture it is done.
If it is too firm flip it back over and cook an additional 5
to 10 minutes. Also, you can poke a sharp knife through
the skin of the upside-down squash. If it slides through

easily, it's probably done. Don't overcook, or it will be mushy.

Procedure:
1. While the squash is cooking, shred the cheese.
2. When squash is finished cooking, use a fork to scrape along sides and bottom to get the spaghetti strands out.
3. Put shredded squash into a colander and squish out as much water as you can.
4. Spread it onto a cookie sheet covered with parchment paper.
5. Cook at 350 degrees for 20 to 30 min (or maybe more) to dry it out. (If you have a lot of squash piled up, you may have to move it around every ten minutes or so to evenly dry it out.)
6. While the squash is in the oven drying out, brown the hamburger in a frying pan. When it's close to browned, put in the cut-up bell pepper and the sliced ripe olives. Add the tomato sauce last.
7. When the squash is finished drying out, mix it with most of the shredded cheese SAVING SOME CHEESE FOR THE TOP to be put on later. Put the squash/cheese combo into a greased pie pan and create a "crust."
8. When the hamburger mixture is heated, pour it into the squash/cheese crust.
9. Cook at 350 degrees for fifteen minutes, then add the last of the cheese on top of the meat mixture.
10. Cook for two or three more minutes to melt the cheese.

Chocolate Cheesecake Pie

Bottom Layer
2/3 cup almond flour
3 tablespoons ground flax
3 tablespoons cacao
2/3 teaspoon baking powder
3 tablespoons sour cream
3 tablespoons melted butter
2 large eggs
½ teaspoon liquid stevia
1 teaspoon vanilla

Cream Cheese Filling
8 ounces cream cheese
8 tablespoons melted butter
4 tablespoons sour cream
½ teaspoon liquid stevia
1 teaspoon vanilla

Procedure (Please note this uses a cake-like bottom layer rather than a traditional pie crust—because Aiden likes it that way.)
1. Pre-heat oven to 350 degrees.
2. Measure out the dry ingredients into a bowl: almond flour, ground flax, cacao, and baking powder.
3. Beat eggs, then add in the melted butter, sour cream, and stevia.
4. Add that to the dry ingredients and mix well with a hand mixer.
5. Spread the batter evenly over the bottom of a greased pie pan.
6. Bake for 12 minutes at 350F. Take pie out and use a

spoon to squish some of the pie up onto the sides of the pie pan.

7. Bake two or three more minutes until a toothpick comes out clean.

8. Let it cool while you work on the cream cheese filling.

Procedure for Cream Cheese Filling

1. Combine cream cheese, butter, sour cream, vanilla, and stevia. Use a hand mixer to mix together well.

2. Plop the cream cheese filling on top of the pie crust and spread evenly with a spoon.

3. Refrigerate before eating to allow it to firm up.